**Gordon Stab**

# In Far Bolivia

**Gordon Stables**

# In Far Bolivia

1st Edition | ISBN: 978-3-75242-754-7

Place of Publication: Frankfurt am Main, Germany

Year of Publication: 2020

Outlook Verlag GmbH, Germany.

Reproduction of the original.

# In Far Bolivia

## A Story of a Strange Wild Land

BY

DR. GORDON STABLES, R.N.

# PREFACE

Every book should tell its own story without the aid of "preface" or "introduction". But as in this tale I have broken fresh ground, it is but right and just to my reader, as well as to myself, to mention prefatorially that, as far as descriptions go, both of the natives and the scenery of Bolivia and the mighty Amazon, my story is strictly accurate.

I trust that Chapter XXIII, giving facts about social life in La Paz and Bolivia, with an account of that most marvellous of all sheets of fresh water in the known world, Lake Titicaca, will be found of general interest.

But vast stretches of this strange wild land of Bolivia are a closed book to the world, for they have never yet been explored; nor do we know aught of the tribes of savages who dwell therein, as far removed from civilization and from the benign influence of Christianity as if they were inhabitants of another planet. I have ventured to send my heroes to this land of the great unknown, and have at the same time endeavoured to avoid everything that might border on sensationalism.

In conclusion, my boys, if spared I hope to take you out with me again to Bolivia in another book, and together we may have stranger adventures than any I have yet told.

THE AUTHOR.

---

# CHAPTER I—ON THE BANKS OF THE GREAT AMAZON

Miles upon miles from the banks of the mighty river, had you wandered far away in the shade of the dark forest that clothed the valleys and struggled high over the mountain-tops themselves, you would have heard the roar and the boom of that great buzz-saw.

As early as six of a morning it would start, or soon after the sun, like a huge red-hot shot, had leapt up from his bed in the glowing east behind the greenery of the hills and woods primeval.

To a stranger coming from the south towards the Amazon—great queen of all the rivers on earth—and not knowing he was on the borders of civilization, the sound that the huge saw made would have been decidedly alarming.

He would have stopped and listened, and listening, wondered. No menagerie of wild beasts could have sent forth a noise so loud, so strange, so persistent! Harsh and low at times, as its great teeth tore through the planks of timber, it would change presently into a dull but dreadful *basso profundo*, such as might have been emitted by antediluvian monsters in the agonies of death or torture, rising anon into a shrill howl or shriek, then subsiding once again into a steady grating roar, that seemed to shake the very earth.

Wild beasts in this black forest heard the sounds, and crept stealthily away to hide themselves in their caves and dens; caymans or alligators heard them too, as they basked in the morning sunshine by lakelet or stream—heard them and crawled away into caves, or took to the water with a sullen plunge that caused the finny inhabitants to dart away in terror to every point of the compass.

"Up with the tree, lads. Feed him home," cried Jake Solomons loudly but cheerily. "Our pet is hungry this morning. I say, Bill, doesn't she look a beauty. Ever see such teeth, and how they shine, too, in the red sunlight. Guess you never did, Bill. I say, what chance would the biggest 'gator that ever crawled have with Betsy here. Why, if Betsy got one tooth in his hide she'd have fifty before you could say 'Jerusalem', and that 'gator'd be cut in two. Tear away, Betsy! Grind and groan and growl, my lass! Have your breakfast, my little pet; why, your voice is sweetest music to my ear. I say, Bill, don't the saw-dust fly a few? I should smile!

"But see," he continued, "yonder come the darkies with our matutinal. Girls and boys with baskets, and I can see the steam curling up under Chloe's arm from the great flagon she is carrying! Look how her white eyes roll, and her white teeth shine as she smiles her six-inch smile! Good girl is Chloe. She knows we're hungry, and that we'll welcome her. Wo, now, Betsy! Let the water off, Bill. Betsy has had her snack, and so we'll have ours."

There was quietness now o'er hill and dell and forest-land.

And this tall Yankee, Jake Solomons, who was fully arrayed in cotton shirt and trousers, his brown arms bare to the shoulder, stretched his splendidly knit but spare form with a sort of a yawn.

"Heigho, Bill!" he said. "I'm pining for breakfast. Aren't you?"

"That I am," replied Burly Bill with his broadest grin.

Jake ran to the open side of the great saw-mill. Three or four strides took him there.

"Ah! Good-morning, Chloe, darling! Morning, Keemo! Morning, Kimo!"

"Mawning, sah!" This was a chorus.

"All along dey blessed good-foh-nuffin boys I no come so queeck," said Chloe.

"Stay, stay, Chloe," cried Jake, "never let your angry passions rise. 'Sides, Chloe, I calculate such language ain't half-proper. But how glittering

4

your cheeks are, Chloe, how white your teeth! There! you smile again. And that vermilion blouse sets off your dark complexion to a nicety, and seems just made for it. Chloe, I would kiss you, but the fear of making Bill jealous holds me back."

Burly Bill shook with laughter. Bill was well named the Burly. Though not so tall as Jake, his frame was immense, though perhaps there was a little more adipose tissue about it than was necessary in a climate like this. But Bill's strength was wonderful. See him, axe in hand, at the foot of a tree! How the chips fly! How set and determined the man's face, while the great beads of sweat stand like pearls on his brow!

Burly Bill was a white man turned black. You couldn't easily have guessed his age. Perhaps he was forty, but at twenty, when still in England, Bill was supple and lithe, and had a skin as white as a schoolboy's. But he had got stouter as the years rolled on, and his face tanned and tanned till it tired of tanning, and first grew purple, and latterly almost black. The same with those hirsute bare arms of his.

There was none of the wild "Ha! ha!" about Bill's laughter. It was a sort of suppressed chuckle, that agitated all his anatomy, the while his merry good-natured eyes sought shelter behind his cheeks' rotundity.

Under a great spreading tree the two men laid themselves down, and Chloe spread their breakfast on a white cloth between them, Jake keeping up his fire of chaff and sweet nothings while she did so. Keemo and Kimo, and the other "good-foh-nuffin boys" had brought their morning meal to the men who fed the great buzz-saw.

"Ah, Chloe!" said Jake, "the odour of that coffee would bring the dead to life, and the fish and the beef and the butter, Chloe! Did you do all this yourself?"

"All, sah, I do all. De boys jes' kick about de kitchen and do nuffin."

"Dear tender-eyed Chloe! How clever you are! Guess you won't be so kind to me when you and I get spliced, eh?"

5

"Ah sah! you no care to marry a poor black gal like Chloe! Dere is a sweet little white missie waiting somew'eres foh Massa Jake. I be your maid, and shine yo' boots till all de samee's Massa Bill's cheek foh true."

As soon as Chloe with her "good-foh-nuffin boys" had cleared away the breakfast things, and retired with a smile and saucy toss of her curly poll, the men lay back and lit their pipes.

"She's a bright intelligent girl that," said Jake. "I don't want a wife or— but I say, Bill, why don't you marry her? I guess she'd make ye a tip-topper."

"Me! Is it marry?"

Burly Bill held back his head and chuckled till he well-nighchoked.

Honest Bill's ordinary English showed that he came from the old country, and more particularly from the Midlands. But Bill could talk properly enough when he pleased, as will soon be seen.

He smoked quietly enough for a time, but every now and then he felt constrained to take his meerschaum from his mouth and give another chuckle or two.

"Tchoo-hoo-hoo!" he laughed. "Me marry! And marry Chloe! Tchoo-hoo-hoo!"

"To change the subject, William," said Jake, "seein' as how you've pretty nearly chuckled yourself silly, or darned near it, how long have you left England?"

"W'y, I coom over with Mr. St. Clair hisse'f, and Roland w'y he weren't more'n seven. Look at 'e now, and dear little Peggy, 'is sister by adoption as ever was, weren't a month over four. Now Rolly 'e bees nigh onto fifteen, and Peggy—the jewel o' the plantation—she's goin' on for twelve, and main tall for that. W'y time do fly! Don't she, Jake?"

"Well, I guess I've been here five years, and durn me if I want to leave. Could we have a better home? I'd like to see it. I'd smile a few odd ones. But listen, why here comes the young 'uns!"

There was the clatter of ponies' feet, and next minute as handsome a boy as ever sat in saddle, and as pretty and bright a lassie as you could wish to meet, galloped into the clearing, and reined up their spirited little steeds close to the spot where the men were lounging.

Burly Bill stuck his thumb into the bowl of his meerschaum to put it out, and Jake threw his pipe on the bank.

Roland was tall for his age, like Peggy. But while a mass of fair and irrepressible hair curled around the boy's sun-burned brow, Peggy's hair was straight and black. When she rode fast it streamed out behind her like pennons in the breeze. What a bright and sunny face was hers too! There was ever a happy smile about her red lips and dark eyes.

"You've got to begin to smoke again immediately," said the boy.

"No, no, Master Roland, not in the presence of your sister."

"But," cried Peggy, with a pretty show of pomposity, "I command you!"

"Ah, then, indeed!" said Jake; and soon both men were blowing clouds that made the very mosquitoes change their quarters.

"Father'll be up soon, riding on Glancer. This nag threw Father, coming home last night. Mind, Glancer is seventeen hands and over."

"He threw him?"

"That he did, in the moonlight. Scared at a 'gator. Father says he heard the 'gator's great teeth snapping and thought he was booked. But lo! Jake, at that very moment Glancer struck out with both hind-legs—you know how he is shod. He smashed the 'gator's skull, and the beast turned up his yellow belly to the moon."

"Bravo!"

"Then Father mounted mighty Glancer and rode quietly home.

"Peggy and I," he continued, "have ridden along the bank to the battlefield to hold a coroner's inquest on the 'gator, but he's been hauled away by his relations. I suppose they'll make potato soup of him."

Burly Bill chuckled.

"Well, Peggy and I are off. See you in the evening, Jake. By-by!"

And away they rode, like a couple of wild Indians, followed by a huge Irish wolf-hound, as faithful a dog to his mistress—for he was Peggy's own pet—as ever dog could be.

They were going to have a day in the forest, and each carried a short six-chambered rifle at the saddle.

A country like the wild one in which they dwelt soon makes anyone brave and fearless. They meant to ride quite a long way to-day and not return till the sun began to decline in the far and wooded west. So, being already quite an old campaigner, Roland had not forgotten to bring luncheon with him, and some for bold Brawn also.

Into the forest they dashed, leaving the mighty river, which was there about fifteen miles broad probably, in their rear.

They knew every pathway of that primeval woodland, and it mattered but little to them that most of these had been worn by the feet of wild beasts. Such tracks wind out and in, and in and out, and meet others in the most puzzling and labyrinthine manner.

Roland carried a compass, and knew how to use it, but the day was unusually fine and sunny, so there was little chance of their getting lost.

The country in which they lived might well have been called the land of perpetual summer.

But at some spots the forest was so pitchy dark, owing to the overhanging trees and wild flowering creepers, that they had to rein up and allow Coz and Boz, as their ponies were named, to cautiously feel the way for themselves.

How far away they might have ridden they could not themselves tell, had they not suddenly entered a kind of fairy glade. At one side it was bounded by a crescentic formation of rock, from the very centre of which spouted a tiny clear crystal waterfall. Beneath was a deep pool, the bottom of which was sand and yellow shingle, with here and there a patch of snow-white quartz. And away from this a little stream went meandering slowly through the glade, keeping it green.

On the other side were the lordly forest trees, bedraped with flowering orchids and ferns.

Flowers and ferns grew here and there in the rockface itself. No wonder the young folks gazed around them in delighted wonder.

Brawn was more practical. He cared nothing for the flowers, but enjoyed to the fullest extent the clear cool water of the crystal pool.

"Oh, isn't it lovely?" said Roland.

"And oh, I am so hungry, Rolly!"

Rolly took the hint.

The ponies were let loose to graze, Brawn being told to head them off if they attempted to take to the woods.

"I understand," said Brawn, with an intelligent glance of his brown eyes and wag of his tail.

Then down the boy and girl squatted with the noble wolf-hound beside them, and Roland speedily spread the banquet on the moss.

I dare say that hunger and romance seldom tread the same platform—at the same time, that is. It is usually one down, the other up; and notwithstanding the extraordinary beauty of their surroundings, for some time both boy and girl applied themselves assiduously to the discussion of the good things before them; that meat-pie disappearing as if by magic. Then the hard-boiled eggs, the well-buttered and flouriest of floury scones, received their attention, and the whole was washed down with *vinum bovis*, as Roland called it, cow's wine, or good milk.

Needless to say, Brawn, whose eyes sparkled like diamonds, and whose ears were conveniently erect, came in for a good share.

Well, but the ponies, Boz and Coz, had not the remotest idea of running away. In fact they soon drew near to the banqueting-table. Coz laid his nose affectionately on his little mistress's shoulder and heaved an equine sigh, and Boz began to nibble at Roland's ears in a very winning way.

And the nibbling and the sigh brought them cakes galore.

Roland offered Boz a bit of pie.

The pony drew back, as if to say, "Vegetarians, weren't you aware?"

But Brawn cocked his bonnie head to one side, knowingly.

"Pitch it this way, master," he said. "I've got a crop for any kind of corn, and a bag for peas."

A strange little rodent creature, much bigger than any rat, however, with beautiful sad-looking eyes, came from the bush, and stood on its hind-legs begging, not a yard away. Its breast was as white as snow.

Probably it had no experience of the genus *homo*, and all the cruelties he is guilty of, under the title of sport.

Roland pitched several pieces of pie towards the innocent. It just tasted a morsel, then back it ran towards the wood with wondrous speed.

If they thought they had seen the last of it, they were much mistaken, for the innocent returned in two minutes time, accompanied not only by another of his own size, but by half a dozen of the funniest little fairies ever seen inside a forest.

"My wife and children," said innocent No. 1.

"My services to you," bobbed innocent No. 2.

But the young ones squawked and squealed, and tumbled and leapt over each other as they fed in a manner so droll that boy and girl had to laugh till the woods rang.

Innocent No. 1 looked on most lovingly, but took not a morsel to himself.

Then all disappeared as suddenly as they had come.

Truly the student of Nature who betakes himself to lonely woods sees many wonders!

It was time now to lie back in the moss and enjoy the *dolce far niente*.

The sky was as blue as blue could be, all between the rifts of slowly-moving clouds. The whisper of the wind among the forest trees, and the murmur of the falling water, came like softest music to Roland's ears. Small wonder, therefore, that his eyes closed, and he was soon in the land of sweet forgetfulness.

But Peggy had a tiny book, from which she read passages to Brawn, who seemed all attention, but kept one eye on the ponies at the sametime.

It was a copy of the "Song of Hiawatha", a poem which Peggy thought ineffably lovely. Hark to her sweet girl voice as she reads:

"These songs so wild and wayward,

These legends and traditions".


They appealed to her simple soul, for dearly did she love the haunts of Nature.

"Loved the sunshine of the meadow,

Loved the shadow of the forest,

Loved the wind among the branches,

The rushing of great rivers

Through their palisades of pine-trees."

She believed, too:

> "That even in savage bosoms
>
> There are longings, yearnings, strivings
>
> For the good they comprehend not;
>
> That feeble hands and helpless,
>
> Groping blindly in the darkness,
>
> Touch God's right hand...
>
> And are lifted up and strengthened".

---

Roland slumbered quietly, and the day went on apace.

He slept so peacefully that she hardly liked to arouse him.

The little red book dropped from her hand and fell on the moss, and her thoughts now went far, far away adown the mighty river that flows so sadly, so solemnly onwards to the great Atlantic Ocean, fed on its way by a hundred rapid streams that melt in its dark bosom and are seen nevermore.

But it was not the river itself the little maiden's thoughts were dwelling on; not the strange wild birds that sailed along its surface on snow-white wings; not the birds of prey—the eagle and the hawk—that hovered high in air, or with eldritch screams darted on their prey like bolts from the blue, and bore their bleeding quarries away to the silent forest; not even the wealth of wild flowers that nodded over the banks of the mighty stream.

Her thoughts were on board a tall and darksome raft that was slowly making its way seaward to distant Pará, or in the boats that towed it. For there was someone on the raft or in those boats who even then might be fondly thinking of the dark-haired maiden he had left behind.

But Peggy's awakening from her dream of romance, and Roland's from his slumber, was indeed a terrible one.

# CHAPTER II—STRANGE ADVENTURES IN THE FOREST—LOST!

Fierce eyes had been watching the little camp for an hour and more, glaring out on the sunny glade from the dark depths of a forest tree not far off; out from under a cloudland of waving foliage that rustled in the balmy wind. Watching, and watching unwaveringly, Peggy, while she read; watching the sleeping Roland; the great wolf-hound, Brawn; and watching the ponies too.

Ever and anon these last would come closer to the tree, as they nibbled grass or moss, then those fierce eyes burned more fiercely, and the cat-like tail of a monster jaguar moved uneasily as if the wild beast meditated a spring.

But the ponies, sniffing danger in the air, perhaps—who can tell?— would toss their manes and retreat to the shadow of the rocks.

Had the dog not been there the beast would have dared all, and sprung at once on one of those nimble steeds.

But he waited and watched, watched and waited, and at long last his time came. With a coughing roar he now launched himself into the air, the elasticity of the branch giving greater force to his spring.

Straight on the shoulders or back of poor Boz he alighted. His talons were well driven home, his white teeth were preparing to tear the flesh from the pony's neck.

Both little steeds yelled wildly, and in nightmarish terror.

Up sprang Brawn, the wolf-hound, and dashed on to the rescue.

Peggy seized her loaded rifle and hurried after him.

Thoroughly awake now, and fully cognizant of the terrible danger, Roland too was quickly on the scene of action.

To fire at a distance were madness. He might have missed the struggling

14

lion and shot poor Boz, or even faithful Brawn.

This enormous dog had seized the beast by one hock, and with his paws against the pony was endeavouring to tear the monster off.

The noise, the movement, the terror, caused poor Roland's head to whirl.

He felt dazed, and almost stupid.

Ah! but Peggy was clear-headed, and a brave and fearless child was she.

Her feet seemed hardly to touch the moss, so lightly did she spring along.

Her little rifle was cocked and ready, and, taking advantage of a few seconds' lull in the fearful scrimmage, she fired at five yards' distance.

The bullet found billet behind the monster's ear, his grip relaxed, and now Brawn tore him easily from his perch and finished him off on the ground, with awful din and habbering.

Then, with blood-dripping jaws he came with his ears lower, half apologetically, to receive the praise and caresses of his master and mistress.

But though the adventure ended thus happily, frightened beyond measure, the ponies, Coz and Boz, had taken to the bush and disappeared.

Knowing well the danger of the situation, Roland and Peggy, with Brawn, tried to follow them. But Irish wolf-hounds have but little scent, and so they searched and searched in vain, and returned at last to the sun-kissed glade.

It was now well on towards three o'clock, and as they had a long forest stretch of at least ten miles before them ere they could touch the banks of the great queen of waters, Roland determined, with the aid of his compass, to strike at once into the beast-trodden pathway by which they had come, and make all haste homewards before the sun should set and darkness envelop the gloomy forest.

"Keep up your heart, Peggy; if your courage and your feet hold out we

15

shall reach the river before dusk."

"I'm not so frightened now," said Peggy; but her lips were very tremulous, and tears stood in her eyes.

"Come, come," she cried, "let us hurry on! Come, Brawn, good dog!"

Brawn leapt up to lick her ear, and taking no thought for the skin of the jaguar, which in more favourable circumstances would have been borne away as a trophy, and proof of Peggy's valour, they now took to the bush in earnest.

Roland looked at his watch.

"Three hours of light and more. Ah! we can do it, if we do not lose our way."

So off they set.

Roland took the lead, rifle in hand, Peggy came next, and brave Brawn brought up the rear.

They were compelled to walk in single file, for the pathways were so narrow in places that two could not have gone abreast.

Roland made constant reference to his little compass, always assuring his companion that they were still heading directly for the river.

They had hurried on for nearly an hour, when Roland suddenly paused.

A huge dark monster had leapt clear and clean across the pathway some distance ahead, and taken refuge in a tree.

It was, no doubt, another jaguar, and to advance unannounced might mean certain death to one of the three.

"Are you all loaded, Peggy?" said Roland.

"Every chamber!" replied the girl.

There was no tremor about her now; and no backwoods Indian could have acted more coolly and courageously.

"Blaze away at that tree then, Peg."

Peggy opened fire, throwing in three or four shots in rapid succession.

The beast, with a terrible cry, darted out of the tree and came rushing along to meet and fight the little party.

"Down, Brawn, down! To heel, sir!"

Next moment Roland fired, and with a terrible shriek the jaguar took to the bush, wounded and bleeding, and was seen no more.

But his yells had awakened the echoes of the forest, and for more than five minutes the din of roaring, growling, and shrieking was fearful.

Wild birds, no doubt, helped to swell the pandemonium.

After a time, however, all was still once more, and the journey was continued in silence.

Even Peggy, usually the first to commence a conversation, felt in no mood for talking now.

She was very tired. Her feet ached, her brow was hot, and her eyes felt as if boiling in their sockets.

Roland had filled his large flask at the little waterfall before leaving the glade, and he now made her drink.

The draught seemed to renew her strength, and she struggled on as bravely as ever.

———————

Just two and a half hours after they had left the forest clearing, and when Roland was holding out hopes that they should soon reach the road by the banks of the river, much to their astonishment they found themselves in a strange clearing which they had never seen before.

The very pathway ended here, and though the boy went round and round the circle, he could find no exit.

To retrace his steps and try to find out the right path was the first thought that occurred to Roland.

This plan was tried, but tried in vain, and so—weary and hopeless now beyond measure—they returned to the centre of the glade and threw themselves down on the soft green moss.

Lost! Lost!

The words kept repeating themselves in poor Roland's brain, but Peggy's fatigue was so complete that she preferred rest even in the midst of danger to going farther.

Brawn, heaving a great sigh, laid himself down beside them.

The warm day wore rapidly to a close, and at last the sun shimmered red through the forest trees.

Then it sank.

The briefest of twilight, and the stars shone out.

Two hours of starlight, then solemnly uprose the round moon and flooded all the glade, draping the whispering trees in a blue glare, beautifully etherealizing them.

Sorrow bringeth sleep.

"Good-night, Rolly! Say your prayers," murmured Peggy.

There were stars in the sky. There were stars too that flitted from bush to bush, while the winds made murmuring music among the lofty branches.

Peggy was repeating to herself lines that she had read that very day:

..."the firefly Wah-wah-tay-see,

Flitting through the dusk of evening,

With the twinkle of its candle,

Lighting up the brakes and bushes.

* * * * *

18

Wah-wah-tay-see, little firefly,

Little, flitting, white-fire insect,

Little dancing, white-fire creature,

Light me with your little candle.

Ere upon my bed I lay me,

Ere in sleep I close my eyelids."

———————

The forest was unusually silent to-night, but ever and anon might be heard some distant growl showing that the woods sheltered the wildest beasts. Or an owl with mournful cry would flap its silent wings as it flew across the clearing.

But nothing waked those tired and weary sleepers.

So the night wore on and on. The moon had reached the zenith, and was shining now with a lustre that almost rivalled daylight itself.

It must have been well on towards two o'clock in the morning when Brawn emitted a low and threatening growl.

This aroused both Roland and Peggy, and the former at once seized his rifle.

Standing there in the pale moonlight, not twenty yards away, was a tall, dark-skinned, and powerful-looking Indian. In his right hand he held a spear or something resembling one; in his left a huge catapult or sling. He was dressed for comfort—certainly not for ornament. Leggings or galligaskins covered his lower extremities, while his body was wrapped in a blanket. He had no head-covering, save a matted mass of hair, in which were stuck a few feathers.

Roland took all this in at a glance as he seized his rifle and prepared for eventualities. According to the traditional painter of Indian life and customs

19

the proper thing for this savage to have said is "Ugh!" He said nothing of the sort. Nor did he give vent to a whoop and yell that would have awakened the wild birds and beasts of the forest and every echo far and near.

"Who goes there?" cried Roland, raising his gun.

"No shootee. No shootee poor Indian man. I friendee you. Plenty friendee."

Probably there was a little romance about Roland, for, instead of saying: "Come this way then, old chap, squat down and give us the news," he said sternly:

"Advance, friend!"

But the Indian stood like a statue.

"No undahstandee foh true."

And Roland had to climb down and say simply:

"Come here, friend, and speak."

Brawn rushed forward now, but he looked a terror, for his hair was all on end like a hyena's, and he growled low but fiercely.

"Down, Brawn! It's a good man, Brawn."

Brawn smelt the Indian's hand, and, seeming satisfied, went back to the spot where Peggy sat wondering and frightened.

She gathered the great dog to her breast and hugged and kissed him.

"What foh you poh chillun sleepee all in de wood so? S'pose wild beas' come eatee you, w'at den you do?"

"But, friend," replied Roland, "we are far from Burnley Hall, our home, and we have lost everything. We have lost our ponies, lost our way, and lost ourselves."

"Poh chillun!" said this strange being. "But now go sleepee foh true. De Indian he lie on blanket. He watchee till de big sun rise."

"Can we trust him, Peggy?"

"Oh yes, yes!" returned Peggy. "He is a dear, good man; I know by his voice."

In ten minutes more the boy and girl were fast asleep.

The Indian watched.

And Brawn watched the Indian.

----

When the sun went down on the previous evening, and there were no signs of the young folks returning, both Mr. St. Clair and his wife became very uneasy indeed.

Then two long hours of darkness ensued before the moon sailed up, first reddening, then silvering, the wavelets and ripples on the great river.

"Surely some evil must have befallen them," moaned Mrs. St. Clair. "Oh, my Roland! my son! I may never see you more. Is there nothing can be done? Tell me! Tell me!"

"We must trust in Providence, Mary; and it is wrong to mourn. I doubt not the children are safe, although perhaps they have lost their way in the woods."

Hours of anxious waiting went by, and it was nearly midnight. The house was very quiet and still, for the servants were asleep.

Burly Bill and Jake had mounted strong horses at moonrise, and gone off to try to find a clue. But they knew it was in vain, nay, 'twould have been sheer madness to enter the forest now. They coo-eed over and over again, but their only answer was the echoing shriek of the wild birds.

They were just about to return after giving their last shrill coo-ee-ee, when out from the moonlit forest, with a fond whinny, sprang Coz and Boz.

Jake sprang out of his saddle, throwing his bridle to Bill.

In the bright moonlight, Jake could see at once that there was something wrong. He placed his hand on Boz's shoulder. He staggered back as he withdrew it.

"Oh, Bill," he cried, "here is blood, and the pony is torn and bleeding! Only a jaguar could have done this. This is terrible."

"Let us return at once," said Bill, who had a right soft heart of his own behind his burly chest.

"But oh!" he added, "how can we break the news to Roland's parents?"

"We'll give them hope. Mrs. St. Clair must know nothing yet, but at early dawn all the ranch must be aroused, and we shall search the forest for miles and miles."

---

Jake, after seeing the ponies safe in their stable, left Bill to look to Boz's wounds, while with St. Clair's leave he himself set off at a round gallop to get assistance from a neighbouring ranch.

Day had not yet broken ere forty good men and true were on the bridle-path and tearing along the river's banks. St. Clair himself was at their head.

I must leave the reader to imagine the joy of all the party when soon after sunrise there emerged from the forest, guided by the strange Indian, Roland, Peggy, and noble Brawn, all looking as fresh as the dew on the tender-eyed hibiscus bloom or the wild flowers that nodded by the river's brim.

"Wirr—rr—r—wouff, wouff, wouff!" barked Brawn, as he bounded forward with joy in every feature of his noble face, and I declare to you there seemed to be a lump in his throat, and the sound of his barking was half-hysterical.

St. Clair could not utter a word as he fondly embraced the children. He pretended to scold a little, but this was all bluff, and simply a ruse to keep back the tears.

But soft-hearted Burly Bill was less successful. He just managed to drop a little to the rear, and it was not once only that he was fain to draw the sleeve of his rough jacket across his eyes.

---

But now they are mounted, and the horses' heads are turned homewards. Peggy is seated in front of Burly Bill, of whom she is very fond, and Roland is saddled with Jake. The Indian and Brawn ran.

Poor Mrs. St. Clair, at the big lawn gate, gazing westward, sees the cavalcade far away on the horizon.

Presently, borne along on the morning breeze come voices raised in a brave and joyous song:

"Down with them, down with the lords of the forest".

And she knows her boy and Peggy are safe.

"Thank God for all his mercies!" she says fervently, then, woman-like, bursts into tears.

# CHAPTER III—BURNLEY HALL, OLD AND NEW

I have noticed more than once that although the life-story of some good old families in England may run long stagnant, still, when one important event does take place, strange thing after strange thing may happen, and the story rushes on with heedless speed, like rippling brooklets to the sea.

The St. Clairs may have been originally a Scottish family, or branch of some Highland clan, but they had been settled on a beautiful estate, far away in the wilds of Cornwall, for over one hundred and fifty years.

Stay, though, we are not going back so far as that. Old history, like old parchment, has a musty odour. Let us come down to more modern times.

When, then, young Roland's grandfather died, and died intestate, the whole of the large estate devolved upon his eldest son, with its fat rentals of fully four thousand a-year. Peggy St. Clair, our little heroine, was his only child, and said to be, even in her infancy, the very image of her dead-and-gone mother.

No wonder her father loved her.

But soon the first great event happened in the life-story of the St. Clairs. For, one sad day Peggy's father was borne home from the hunting-field grievously wounded.

All hope of recovery was abandoned by the doctor shortly after he had examined his patient.

Were Herbert to die intestate, as his father had done, his second brother John, according to the old law, could have stepped into his shoes and become lord of Burnley Hall and all its broad acres.

But, alive to the peril of his situation, which the surgeon with tears in his eyes pointed out to him, the dying man sent at once for his solicitor, and a will was drawn up and placed in this lawyer's hands, and moreover he was appointed one of the executors. This will was to be kept in a safe until Peggy should be seventeen years of age, when it was to be opened and read.

I must tell you that between the brothers Herbert and John there had long existed a sort of blood-feud, and it was as well they never met.

Thomas, however, was quickly at his wounded brother's bedside, and never left it until—

"Clay-cold Death had closed his eye".

The surgeon had never given any hopes, yet during the week that intervened between the terrible accident and Herbert's death there were many hours in which the doomed man appeared as well as ever, though scarce able to move hand or foot. His mind was clear at such times, and he talked much with Thomas about the dear old times when all were young.

Up till now this youngest son and brother, Thomas, had led rather an uneasy and eventful life. Nothing prospered with him, though he had tried most things.

He was married, and had the one child, Roland, to whom the reader has already been introduced.

"Now, dear Tom," said Herbert, one evening after he had lain still with closed eyes for quite a long time, and he placed a white cold hand in that of his brother as he spoke, "I am going to leave you. We have always been good friends and loved each other well. All I need tell you now, and I tell you in confidence, is that Peggy, at the age of seventeen, will be my heir, with you, dear Tom, as her guardian."

Tom could not reply for the gathering tears. He just pressed Herbert's hand in silence.

"Well," continued the latter, "things have not gone over well with you, I know, but I have often heard you say you could do capitally if you emigrated to an almost new land—a land you said figuratively 'flowing with milk and honey'. I confess I made no attempt to assist you to go to the great valley of the Amazon. It was for a selfish reason I detained you. My brother John being nobody to me, my desire was to have you near."

He paused, almost exhausted, and Tom held a little cup of wine to his lips.

Presently he spoke again.

"My little Peggy!" he moaned. "Oh, it is hard, hard to leave my darling!"

"Tom, listen. You are to take Peggy to your home. You are to care for her as the apple of your eye. You must be her father, your wife her mother."

"I will! I will! Oh, brother, can you doubt me!"

"No, no, Tom. And now you may emigrate. I leave you thirty thousand pounds, all my deposit account at Messrs. Bullion & Co.'s bank. This is for Peggy and you. My real will is a secret at present, and that which will be read after—I go, is a mere epitome. But in future it will be found that I have not forgotten even John."

Poor Peggy had run in just then, and perched upon the bed, wondering much that her father should lie there so pale and still, and make no attempt to romp with her. At this time her hair was as yellow as the first approach of dawn in the eastern sky.

---

That very week poor Squire St. Clair breathed his last.

John came to the funeral with a long face and a crape-covered hat, looking more like a mute than anything else.

He sipped his wine while the epitomized will was read; but a wicked

26

light flashed from his eyes, and he ground out an oath at its conclusion.

All the information anyone received was that though sums varying from five hundred pounds to a thousand were left as little legacies to distant relations and to John, as well as *douceurs* to the servants, the whole of the estates were willed in a way that could not be divulged for many a long year.

John seized his hat, tore from it the crape, and dashed it on the floor. The crape on his arm followed suit. He trampled on both and strode away slamming the door behind him.

Years had flown away.

Tom and his wife had emigrated to the banks of the Amazon. They settled but a short time at or near one of its mouths, and then Tom, who had no lack of enterprise, determined to journey far, far into the interior, where the land was not so level, where mountains nodded to the moon, and giant forests stretched illimitably to the southward and west.

At first Tom and his men, with faithful Bill as overseer, were mere squatters, but squatters by the banks of the queen of waters, and in a far more lovely place than dreams of elfinland. Labour was very cheap here, and the Indians soon learned from the white men how to work.

Tom St. Clair had imported carpenters and artificers of many sorts from the old country, to say nothing of steam plant and machinery, and that great resounding steel buzz-saw.

Now, although not really extravagant, he had an eye for the beautiful, and determined to build himself a house and home that, although not costing a deal, would be in reality a miniature Burnley Hall. And what a truly joyous time Peggy and her cousin, or adopted brother, had of it while the house was gradually being built by the busy hands of the trained Indians and their white brethren!

Not they alone, but also a boy called Dick Temple, whose uncle was Tom St. Clair's nearest neighbour, That is, he lived a trifle over seven miles higher up the river. Dick was about the same age and build as Roland.

There was a good road between Temple's ranch and Tom St. Clair's place, and when, after a time, Tom and Peggy had a tutor imported for their own especial benefit, the two families became very friendly indeed.

Dick Temple was a well-set-up and really brave and good-looking lad. Little Peggy averred that there never had been, or never could be, another boy half so nice as Dick.

But I may as well state here at once and be done with it—Dick was simply a reckless, wild dare-devil. Nothing else would suffice to describe young Dick's character even at this early age. And he soon taught Roland to be as reckless as himself.

———

Time rolled on, and the new Burnley Hall was a *fait accompli.*

The site chosen by Tom for his home by the river was a rounded and wooded hill about a quarter of a mile back from the immediate bank of the stream. But all the land between the hill and the Amazon was cultivated, and not only this, but up and down the river as well for over a mile, for St. Clair wanted to avoid too close contact with unfriendly alligators, and these scaly reptiles avoid land on which crops are growing.

The tall trees were first and foremost cleared off the hill; not all though. Many of the most beautiful were left for effect, not to say shade, and it was pleasant indeed to hear the wind whispering through their foliage, and the bees murmuring in their branches, in this flowery land of eternal summer.

Nor was the undergrowth of splendid shrubs and bushes and fruit-trees cleared away. They were thinned, however, and beautiful broad winding walks led up through them towards the mansion.

The house was one of many gables; altogether English, built of quartz for the most part, and having a tower to it of great height.

From this tower one could catch glimpses of the most charming scenery, up and down the river, and far away on the other shore, where forests swam in the liquid air and giant hills raised their blue tops far into the sky.

So well had Tom St. Clair flourished since taking up his quarters here that his capital was returning him at least one hundred per cent, after allowing for wear and tear of plant.

I could not say for certain how many white men he had with him. The number must have been close on fifty, to say nothing of the scores and scores of Indians.

Jake Solomons and Burly Bill were his overseers, but they delighted in hard work themselves, as we have already seen. So, too, did Roland's father himself, and as visitors to the district were few, you may be certain he never wore a London hat nor evening dress.

Like those of Jake and Bill, his sleeves were always rolled up, and his muscular arms and brave square face showed that he was fit for anything. No, a London hat would have been sadly out of place; but the broad-brimmed Buffalo Bill he wore became him admirably.

That big buzz-saw was a triumph. The clearing of the forest commenced from close under the hill where stood the mansion, and strong horses and bullocks were used to drag the gigantic trees towards the mill.

Splendid timber it was!

No one could have guessed the age of these trees until they were cut down and sawn into lengths, when their concentric rings might be counted.

The saw-mill itself was a long way from the mansion-house, with the villages for the whites and Indians between, but quite separate from each other.

The habitations of the whites were raised on piles well above the somewhat damp ground, and steps led up to them. Two-roomed most of them were, but that of Jake was of a more pretentious character. So, too, was Burly Bill's hut.

It would have been difficult to say what the Indians lived on. Cakes, fruit, fish, and meat of any kind might form the best answer to the question. They ate roasted snakes with great relish, and many of these were of the deadly-poisonous class. The heads were cut off and buried first, however, and thus all danger was prevented. Young alligators were frequently caught, too, and made into a stew.

The huts these faithful creatures lived in were chiefly composed of bamboo, timber, and leaves. Sometimes they caught fire. That did not trouble the savages much, and certainly did not keep them awake at night. For, had the whole village been burned down, they could have built another in a surprisingly short time.

When our hero and heroine got lost in the great primeval forest, Burnley Hall was in the most perfect and beautiful order, and its walks, its flower-garden, and shrubberies were a most pleasing sight. All was under the superintendence of a Scotch gardener, whom St. Clair had imported for the purpose.

By this time, too, a very large portion of the adjoining forest had been cut down, and the land on which those lofty trees had grown was under cultivation.

If the country which St. Clair had made his home was not in reality a land flowing with milk and honey, it yielded many commodities equally valuable. Every now and then—especially when the river was more or less in flood—immense rafts were sent down stream to distant Pará, where the valuable timber found ready market.

Several white men in boats always went in charge of these, and the boats served to assist in steering, and towing as well.

These rafts used often to be built close to the river before an expected rising of the stream, which, when it did come, floated them off and away.

But timber was not the only commodity that St. Clair sent down from his great estate. There were splendid quinine-trees. There was coca and cocoa, too.

There was a sugar plantation which yielded the best results, to say nothing of coffee and tobacco, Brazil-nuts and many other kinds of nuts, and last, but not least, there was gold.

This latter was invariably sent in charge of a reliable white man, and St. Clair lived in hope that he would yet manage to position a really paying gold-mine.

More than once St. Clair had permitted Roland and Peggy to journey down to Pará on a great raft. But only at the season when no storms blew. They had an old Indian servant to cook and "do" for them, and the centre of the raft was hollowed out into a kind of cabin roofed over with bamboo and leaves. Steps led up from this on to a railed platform, which was called the deck.

Burly Bill would be in charge of boats and all, and in the evenings he would enter the children's cabin to sing them songs and tell them strange, weird tales of forest life.

He had a banjo, and right sweetly could he play. Old Beeboo the Indian, would invariably light his meerschaum for him, smoking it herself for a good five minutes first and foremost, under pretence of getting it well alight.

Beeboo, indeed, was altogether a character. Both Mr. and Mrs. St. Clair liked her very much, however, for she had been in the family, and nursed both Peggy and Roland, from the day they had first come to the country. As for her age, she might have been any age between five-and-twenty and one hundred and ten. She was dark in skin—oh, no! not black, but more of copper colour, and showed a few wrinkles at early morn. But when Beeboo was figged out in her nicest white frock and her deep-blue or crimson blouse, with her hair hanging down in two huge plaits, then, with the smile that always hovered around her lips and went dancing away up her face till it flickered about her eyes, she was very pleasant indeed. The wrinkles had all flown up to the moon or somewhere, and Beeboo was five-and-twenty once again.

I must tell you something, however, regarding her, and that is the worst. Beeboo came from a race of cannibals who inhabit one of the wildest and almost inaccessible regions of Bolivia, and her teeth had been filed by flints into a triangular shape, the form best adapted for tearing flesh. She had been brought thence, along with a couple of wonderful monkeys and several parrots, when only sixteen, by an English traveller who had intended to make her a present to his wife.

Beeboo never got as far as England, however. She had watched her chance, and one day escaped to the woods, taking with her one of the monkeys, who was an especial favourite with this strange, wild girl.

She was frequently seen for many years after this. It was supposed she had lived on roots and rats—I'm not joking—and slept at night in trees. She managed to clothe herself, too, with the inner rind of the bark of certain shrubs. But how she had escaped death from the talons of jaguars and other wild beasts no one could imagine.

Well, one day, shortly after the arrival of St. Clair, hunters found the jaguar queen, as they called her, lying in the jungle at the foot of a tree.

There was a jaguar not far off, and a huge piece of sodden flesh lay near Beeboo's cheek, undoubtedly placed there by this strange, wild pet, while close beside her stood a tapir.

Beeboo was carried to the nearest village, and the tapir followed as gently as a lamb. My informant does not know what became of the tapir, but Beeboo was tamed, turned a Christian too, and never evinced any inclination to return to the woods.

Yet, strangely enough, no puma nor jaguar would ever even growl or snarl at Beeboo.

These statements can all be verified.

# CHAPTER IV—AWAY DOWN THE RIVER

Before we start on this adventurous cruise, let us take a peep at an upland region to the south of the Amazon. It was entirely surrounded by caoutchouc or india-rubber trees, and it was while wandering through this dense forest with Jake, and making arrangements for the tapping of those trees, the juice of which was bound to bring the St. Clairs much money, that they came upon the rocky table-land where they found the gold.

This was some months after the strange Indian had found the "babes in the wood", as Jake sometimes called Roland and Peggy.

"I say, sir, do you see the quartz showing white everywhere through the bloom of those beautiful flowers?"

"Ugh!" cried St. Clair, as a splendidly-coloured but hideous large snake hissed and glided away from between his feet. "Ugh! had I tramped on that fellow my prospecting would have been all ended."

"True, sir," said Jake; "but about the quartz?"

"Well, Jake."

"Well, Mr. St. Clair, there is gold here. I do not say that we've struck an El Dorado, but I am certain there is something worth digging for in this region."

"Shall we try? You've been in Australia. What say you to a shaft?"

"Good! But a horizontal shaft carried into the base of this hill or hummock will, I think, do for the present. It is only for samples, you know."

And these samples had turned out so well that St. Clair, after claiming the whole hill, determined to send Jake on a special message to Pará to establish a company for working it.

He could take no more labour on his own head, for really he had more than enough to do with his estate.

No white men were allowed to work at the shaft. Only Indians, and these were housed on the spot. So that the secret was well kept.

And now the voyage down the river was to be undertaken, and a most romantic cruise it turned out to be.

St. Clair had ordered a steamer to be built for him in England and sent out in pieces. She was called *The Peggy*, after our heroine. Not very large— but little over the dimensions of a large steam-launch, in fact—but big enough for the purpose of towing along the immense raft with the aid of the current.

Jake was to go with his samples of golden sand and his nuggets; Burly Bill, also, who was captain of the *Peggy*; and Beeboo, to attend to the youngsters in their raft saloon. Brawn was not to be denied; and last, but not least, went wild Dick Temple.

The latter was to sleep on board the steamer, but he would spend most of his time by day on the raft.

All was ready at last. The great raft was floated and towed out far from the shore. All the plantation hands, both whites and Indians, were gathered on the banks, and gave many a lusty cheer as the steamer and raft got under way.

The last thing that those on shore heard was the sonorous barking of the great wolf-hound, Brawn.

There was a ring of joy in it, however, that brought hope to the heart of both Tom St. Clair and his winsome wife.

Well, to our two heroes and to Peggy, not to mention Brawn and Burly Bill, the cruise promised to be all one joyous picnic, and they set themselves to make the most of it.

But to Jake Solomons it presented a more serious side. He was St. Clair's representative and trusted man, and his business was of the highest importance, and would need both tact and skill.

However, there was a long time to think about all this, for the river does not run more than three miles an hour, and although the little steamer could hurry the raft along at probably thrice that speed, still long weeks must elapse before they could reach their destination.

As far as the raft was concerned, this would not be Pará. She would be grounded near to a town far higher up stream, and the timber, nuts, spices, and rubber taken seaward by train.

In less than two days everyone had settled down to the voyage.

The river was very wide and getting wider, and soon scarcely could they see the opposite shore, except as a long low green cloud on the northern horizon.

Life on board the raft was for a whole week a most uneventful dreamy sort of existence. One day was remarkably like another. There was the blue of the sky above, the blue on the river's great breast, broken, however, by thousands of lines of rippling silver.

There were strangely beautiful birds flying tack and half-tack around the steamer and raft, waving trees flower-bedraped—the flowers trailing and creeping and climbing everywhere, and even dipping their sweet faces in the water,—flowers of every hue of the rainbow.

Dreamy though the atmosphere was, I would not have you believe that our young folks relapsed into a state of drowsy apathy. Far from it. They were very happy indeed. Dick told Peggy that their life, or his, felt just like some beautiful song-waltz, and that he was altogether so happy and jolly that he had sometimes to turn out in the middle watch to laugh.

Peggy had not to do that.

In her little state-room on one side of the cabin, and in a hammock, she slept as soundly as the traditional top, and on a grass mat on the deck, with a footstool for a pillow, slumbered Beeboo.

Roland slept on the other side, and Brawn guarded the doorway at the foot of the steps.

Long before Peggy was awake, and every morning of their aquatic lives, the dinghy boat took the boys a little way out into mid-stream, and they stripped and dived, enjoyed a two-minutes' splash, and got quickly on board again.

The men always stood by with rifles to shoot any alligator that might be seen hovering nigh, and more than once reckless Dick had a narrow escape.

"But," he said one day in his comical way, "one has only once to die, you know, and you might as well die doing a good turn as any other way."

"Doing a good turn?" said Roland enquiringly.

"Certainly. Do you not impart infinite joy to a cayman if you permit him to eat you?"

The boys were always delightfully hungry half an hour before breakfast was served.

And it was a breakfast too!

Beeboo would be dressed betimes, and have the cloth laid in the saloon. The great raft rose and fell with a gentle motion, but there was nothing to hurt, so that the dishes stuck on the cloth without any guard.

Beeboo could bake the most delicious of scones and cakes, and these, served up hot in a clean white towel, were most tempting; the butter was of the best and sweetest. Ham there was, and eggs of the gull, with fresh fried fish every morning, and fragrant coffee.

Was it not quite idyllic?

The forenoon would be spent on deck under the awning; there was plenty to talk about, and books to read, and there was the ever-varying panorama to gaze upon, as the raft went smoothly gliding on, and on, and on.

Sometimes they were in very deep water close to the bank, for men were always in the chains taking soundings from the steamer's bows.

Close enough to admire the flowers that draped the forest trees; close enough to hear the wild lilt of birds or the chattering of monkeys and parrots; close enough to see tapirs moving among the trees, watched, often enough, by the fierce sly eyes of ghastly alligators, that flattened themselves against rocks or bits of clay soil, looking like a portion of the ground, but warily waiting until they should see a chance to attack.

There cannot be too many tapirs, and there cannot be too few alligators. So our young heroes thought it no crime to shoot these squalid horrors wherever seen.

But one forenoon clouds banked rapidly up in the southern sky, and soon the sun was hidden in sulphurous rolling banks of cumulus.

No one who has ever witnessed a thunderstorm in these regions can live long enough to forget it.

For some time before it came on the wind had gone down completely. In yonder great forest there could not have been breeze or breath enough to stir the pollen on the trailing flowers. The sun, too, seemed shorn of its beams, the sky was no longer blue, but of a pale saffron or sulphur colour.

It was then that giant clouds, like evil beasts bent on havoc and destruction, began to show head above the horizon. Rapidly they rose, battalion on battalion, phalanx on phalanx.

There were low mutterings even now, and flashes of fire in the far distance. But it was not until the sky was entirely overcast that the storm came on in dread and fearful earnest. At this time it was so dark, that down in the raft saloon an open book was barely visible. Then peal after peal, and vivid flash after flash, of blue and crimson fire lit up forest and stream, striking our heroes and heroine blind, or causing their eyes for a time to overrun with purple light.

So terrific was the thunder that the raft seemed to rock and shiver in the sound.

This lasted for fully half an hour, the whole world seeming to be in flames.

Peggy stood by Dick on the little deck, and he held her arm in his; held her hand too, for it was cold and trembling.

"Are you afraid?" he whispered, during a momentary lull.

"No, Dick, not afraid, only cold, so cold; take me below."

He did so.

He made her lie down on the little sofa, and covered her with a rug.

All just in time, for now down came the awful rain. It was as if a water-spout had broken over the seemingly doomed raft, and was sinking it below the dark waters of the river.

Luckily the boys managed to batten down in time, or the little saloon would have been flooded.

They lit the lamp, too.

But with the rain the storm seemed to increase in violence, and a strong wind had arisen and added greatly to the terror of the situation. Hail came down as large as marbles, and the roaring and din was now deafening and terrible.

Then, the wind ceased to blow almost instantaneously. It did not die away. It simply dropped all of a sudden. Hail and rain ceased shortly after.

Dick ventured to peep on deck.

It was still dark, but far away and low down on the horizon a streak of the brightest blue sky that ever he had seen had made its appearance. It broadened and broadened as the dark canopy of clouds, curtain-like, was lifted.

"Come up, Peggy. Come up, Rol. The storm is going. The storm has almost gone," cried Dick; and soon all three stood once more on the deck.

Away, far away over the northern woods rolled the last bank of clouds, still giving voice, however, still spitting fire.

But now the sun was out and shining brightly down with a heat that was fierce, and the raft was all enveloped in mist.

So dense, indeed, was the fog that rose from the rain-soaked raft, that all the scenery was entirely obscured. It was a hot vapour, too, and far from pleasant, so no one was sorry when Burly Bill suddenly appeared from the lower part of the raft.

"My dear boys," he said heartily, "why, you'll be parboiled if you stop here. Come with me, Miss Peggy, and you, Brawn; I'll come back for you, lads. Don't want to upset the dinghy all among the 'gators, see?"

Bill was back again in a quarter of an hour, and the boys were also taken on board the boat.

"She's a right smart little boat as ever was," said Bill; "but if we was agoin' to get 'er lip on to the water, blow me tight, boys, if the 'gators wouldn't board us. They'm mebbe very nice sociable kind o' animals, but bust my buttons if I'd like to enter the next world down a 'gator's gullet."

Beeboo did not mind the steam a bit, and by two o'clock she had as nice a dinner laid in the raft saloon as ever boy or girl sat down to.

But by this time the timbers were dry once more, and although white clouds of fog still lay over the low woods, all was now bright and cheerful. Yet not more so than the hearts of our brave youngsters.

Courage and sprightliness are all a matter of strength of heart, and you cannot make yourself brave if your system is below par. The coward is really more to be pitied than blamed.

Well, it was very delightful, indeed, to sit on deck and talk, build castles in the air, and dream daydreams.

The air was cool and bracing now, and the sun felt warm, but by no means too hot.

The awning was prettily lined with green cloth, the work of Mrs. St. Clair's own hands, assisted by the indefatigable Beeboo, and there was not anything worth doing that she could not put willing, artful hands to.

The awning was scalloped, too, if that be the woman's word for the flaps that hung down a whole foot all round. "Vandyked" is perhaps more correct, but then, you see, the sharp corners of the vandyking were all rounded off. So I think scalloped must stand, though the word reminds me strangely of oysters.

But peeping out from under the scalloped awning, and gazing northwards across the sea-like river, boats under steam could be noticed. Passengers on board too, both ladies and gentlemen, the former all rigged out in summer attire.

"Would you like to be on board yonder?" said Dick to Peggy, as the girl handed him back the lorgnettes.

"No, indeed, I shouldn't," she replied, with a saucy toss of her pretty head.

"Well," she added, "if you were there, little Dickie, I mightn't mind it so much."

"Little Dick! Eh?" Dick laughed right heartily now.

"Yes, little Dickie. Mind, I am nearly twelve; and after I'm twelve I'm in my teens, quite an old girl. A child no longer anyhow. And after I'm in my teens I'll soon be sixteen, and then I suppose I shall marry."

"Who will marry you, Peggy?"

This was not very good grammar, but Dick was in downright earnest anyhow, and his young voice had softened wonderfully.

"Me?" he added, as she remained silent, with her eyes seeming to follow the rolling tide.

"You, Dick! Why, you're only a child!"

"Why, Peggy, I'm fifteen—nearly, and if I live I'm bound to get older and bigger."

"No, no, Dick, you can marry Beeboo, and I shall get spliced, as the sailors call it, to Burly Bill."

The afternoon wore away, and Beeboo came up to summon "the chillun" to tea.

Up they started, forgetting all about budding love, flirtation, and future marriages, and made a rush for the companion-ladder.

"Wowff—wowff!" barked Brawn, and the 'gators on shore and the tapirs in the woods lifted heads to listen, while parrots shrieked and monkeys chattered and scolded among the lordly forest trees.

"Wowff—wowff!" he barked. "Who says cakes and butter?"

The night fell, and Burly Bill came on board with his banjo, and his great bass voice, which was as sweet as the tone of a 'cello.

Bill was funnier than usual to-night, and when Beeboo brought him a big tumbler of rosy rum punch, made by herself and sweetened with honey, he was merrier still.

Then to complete his happiness Beeboo lit his pipe.

She puffed away at it for some time as usual, by way of getting it in working order.

"'Spose," she said, "Beeboo not warm de bowl ob de big pipe plenty proper, den de dear chile Bill take a chill."

"You're a dear old soul, Beeb," said Bill.

Then the dear old soul carefully wiped the amber mouth-piece with her apron, and handed Burly Bill his comforter.

The great raft swayed and swung gently to and fro, so Bill sang his pet sea-song, "The Rose of Allandale". He was finishing that bonnie verse—

"My life had been a wilderness,

Unblest by fortune's gale,

Had fate not linked my lot to hers,

The Rose of Allandale",

when all at once an ominous grating was heard coming from beneath the raft, and motion ceased as suddenly as did Bill's song.

"Save us from evil!" cried Bill. "The raft is aground!"

# CHAPTER V—A DAY IN THE FOREST WILDS

Burly Bill laid down his banjo. Then he pushed his great extinguisher of a thumb into the bowl of his big meerschaum, and arose.

"De good Lawd ha' mussy on our souls, chillun!" cried Beeboo, twisting her apron into a calico rope. "We soon be all at de bottom ob de deep, and de 'gators a-pickin' de bones ob us!"

"Keep quiet, Beeb, there's a dear soul! Never a 'gator'll get near you. W'y, look 'ow calm Miss Peggy is. It be'ant much as'll frighten she."

Burly Bill could speak good English when he took time, but invariably reverted to Berkshire when in the least degree excited.

He was soon on board the little steamer.

"What cheer, Jake?" he said.

"Not much o' that. A deuced unlucky business. May lose the whole voyage if it comes on to blow!"

"W'y, Jake, lad, let's 'ope for the best. No use givin' up; be there? I wouldn't let the men go to prayers yet awhile, Jake. Not to make a bizness on't like, I means."

Well, the night wore away, but the raft never budged, unless it was to get a firmer hold of the mud and sand.

A low wind had sprung up too, and if it increased to a gale she would soon begin to break up.

It was a dreary night and a long one, and few on board the steamer slept a wink.

But day broke at last, and the sun's crimson light changed the ripples on the river from leaden gray to dazzling ruby.

Then the wind fell.

"There are plenty of river-boats, Bill," said Jake. "What say you to intercept one and ask assistance?"

"Bust my buttons if I would cringe to ne'er a one on 'em! They'd charge salvage, and sponge enormous. I knows the beggars as sails these puffin' Jimmies well."

"Guess you're about right, Bill, and you know the river better'n I."

"Listen, Jake. The bloomin' river got low all at once, like, after the storm, and so you got kind o' befoozled, and struck. I'd a-kept further out. But Burly Bill ain't the man to bully his mate. On'y listen again. The river'll rise in a day or two, and if the wind keeps in its sack, w'y we'll float like a thousand o' bricks on an old Thames lumper! Bust my buttons, Jake, if we don't!"

"Well, Bill, I don't know anything about the bursting of your buttons, but you give me hope. So I'll go to breakfast. Tell the engineer to keep the fires banked."

Two days went past, and never a move made the raft.

It was a wearisome time for all. The "chillun", as Beeboo called them, tried to beguile it in the best way they could with reading, talking, and deck games.

Dick and Roland were "dons" at leap-frog, and it mattered not which of them was giving the back, but as soon as the other leapt over Brawn followed suit, greatly to the delight of Peggy. He jumped in such a business-like way that everybody was forced to laugh, especially when the noble dog took a leap that would have cleared a five-barred gate.

But things were getting slow on the third morning, when up sprang Burly Bill with his cartridge-belt on and his rifle under his arm.

"Cap'n Jake," he said, touching his cap in Royal Navy fashion, "presents his compliments to the crew of this durned old stack o' timber, and begs to

44

say that Master Rolly and Master Dick can come on shore with me for a run among the 'gators, but that Miss Peggy had better stop on board with Beeboo. Her life is too precious to risk!"

"Precious or not precious," pouted the girl, "Miss Peggy's going, and Brawn too; so you may tell Captain Jake that."

"Bravo, Miss Peggy! you're a real St. Clair. Well, Beeboo, hurry up, and get the nicest bit of cold luncheon ready for us ever you made in your life."

"Beeboo do dat foh true. Plenty quick, too; but oh, Massa Bill, 'spose you let any ebil ting befall de poh chillun, I hopes de 'gators'll eat you up!"

"More likely, Beeb, that we'll eat them; and really, come to think of it, a slice off a young 'gator's tail aint 'arf bad tackle, Beeboo."

An hour after this the boat was dancing over the rippling river. It was not the dinghy, but a gig. Burly Bill himself was stroke, and three Indians handled the other bits of timber, while Roland took the tiller.

The redskins sang a curious but happy boat-lilt as they rowed, and Bill joined in with his 'cello voice:

"Ober de watter and ober de sea—ee—ee,

De big black boat am rowing so free,

    Eee—Eee—O—ay—O!

De big black boat, is it nuffin' to me—ee—ee,

We're rowing so free?

"Oh yes, de black boat am some-dings to me

As she rolls o'er de watter and swings o'er de sea,

Foh de light ob my life, she sits in de stern,

An' sweet am de glance o' Peggy's dark e'e,

    Ee—ee—O—ay—O—O!"

"Well steered!" said Burly Bill, as Roland ran the gig on the sandy beach of a sweet little backwater.

Very soon all were landed. Bill went first as guide, and the Indians brought up the rear, carrying the basket and a spare gun or two.

Great caution and care were required in venturing far into this wild, tropical forest, not so much on account of the beasts that infested it as the fear of getting lost.

It was very still and quiet here, however, and Bill had taken the precaution to leave a man in the boat, with orders to keep his weather ear "lifting", and if he heard four shots fired in rapid succession late in the afternoon to fire in reply at once.

It was now the heat of the day, however, and the hairy inhabitants of this sylvan wilderness were all sound asleep, jaguars and pumas among the trees, and the tapirs in small herds wherever the jungle was densest.

There was no chance, therefore, of getting a shot at anything. Nevertheless, the boys and Peggy were not idle. They had brought butterfly-nets with them, and the specimens they caught when about five miles inland, where the forest opened out into a shrub-clad moorland, were large and glorious in the extreme.

Indeed, some of them would fetch gold galore in the London markets.

But though these butterflies had an immense spread of quaintly-shaped and exquisitely-coloured wings, the smaller ones were even more brilliant.

Strange it is that Nature paints these creatures in colours which no sunshine can fade. All the tints that man ever invented grow pale in the sun; these never do, and the same may be said concerning the tropical birds that they saw so many of to-day.

But no one had the heart to shoot any of these. Why should they soil such beautiful plumage with blood, and so bring grief and woe into this love-lit wilderness?

This is not a book on natural history, else gladly would I describe the beauties in shape and colour of the birds, and their strange manners, the wary ways adopted in nest-building, and their songs and queer ways of love-making.

Suffice it to say here that the boys were delighted with all the tropical wonders and all the picturesque gorgeousness they saw everywhere around them.

But their journey was not without a spice of real danger and at times of discomfort. The discomfort we may dismiss at once. It was borne, as Beeboo would say, with Christian "forty-tood", and was due partly to the clouds of mosquitoes they encountered wherever the soil was damp and marshy, and partly to the attacks of tiny, almost invisible, insects of the jigger species that came from the grass and ferns and heaths to attack their legs.

Burly Bill was an old forester, and carried with him an infallible remedy for mosquito and jigger bites, which acted like a charm.

In the higher ground—where tropical heath and heather painted the surface with hues of crimson, pink, and purple—snakes wriggled and darted about everywhere.

One cannot help wondering why Nature has taken the pains to paint many of the most deadly of these in colours that rival the hues of the humming-birds that yonder flit from bush to bush, from flower to flower.

Perhaps it is that they may the more easily seek their prey, their gaudy coats matching well with the shrubs and blossoms that they wriggle amongst, while gliding on and up to seize helpless birds in their nests or to devour the eggs.

Parrots here, and birds of that ilk, have an easy way of repelling such invaders, for as soon as they see them they utter a scream that paralyses the intruders, and causes them to fall helplessly to the ground.

To all creatures Nature grants protection, and clothes them in a manner that shall enable them to gain a subsistence; but, moreover, every creature in the world has received from the same great power the means of defending or protecting itself against the attacks of enemies.

On both sides, then, is Nature just, for though she does her best to keep living species extant until evolved into higher forms of life, she permits each species to prey on the overgrowth or overplus of others that it may live.

Knocking over a heap of soft dry mould with the butt end of his rifle, Dick started back in terror to see crawl out from the heap a score or more of the most gigantic beetles anyone could imagine. These were mostly black, or of a beautiful bronze, with streaks of metallic blue and crimson.

They are called harlequins, and live on carrion. Nothing that dies comes wrong to these monsters, and a few of them will seize and carry away a dead snake five or six hundred times their own weight. My readers will see by this that it is not so much muscle that is needed for feats of strength as indomitable will and nerve force. But health must be at the bottom of all. Were a man, comparatively speaking, as strong as one of these beetles, he could lift on his back and walk off with a weight of thirty tons!

Our heroes had to stop every now and then to marvel at the huge working ants, and all the wondrous proofs of reason they evinced.

It was well to stand off, however, if, with snapping horizontal mandibles and on business intent, any of these fellows approached. For their bites are as poisonous as those of the green scorpions or centipedes themselves.

What with one thing or another, all hands were attacked by healthy hunger at last, and sought the shade of a great spreading tree to satisfy Nature's demands.

When the big basket was opened it was found that Beeboo had quite excelled herself. So glorious a luncheon made every eye sparkle to look at it.

And the odour thereof caused Brawn's mouth to water and his eyes to sparkle with expectancy.

The Indians had disappeared for a time. They were only just round the shoulder of a hill, however, where they, too, were enjoying a good feed.

But just as Burly Bill was having a taste from a clear bottle, which, as far as the look of it went, would have passed for cold tea, two Indian boys appeared, bringing with them the most delicious of fruits as well as fresh ripe nuts.

The luncheon after that merged into a banquet.

Burly Bill took many sips of his cold tea. When I come to think over it, however, I conclude there was more rum than cold tea in that brown mixture, or Bill would hardly have smacked his lips and sighed with such satisfaction after every taste.

The fruit done, and even Brawn satisfied, the whole crew gave themselves up to rest and meditation. The boys talked low, because Peggy's meditations had led to gentle slumber. An Indian very thoughtfully brought a huge plantain leaf which quite covered her, and protected her from the chequered rays of sunshine that found their way through the tree. Brawn edged in below the leaf also, and enjoyed a good sleep beside his little mistress.

Not a gun had been fired all day long, yet a more enjoyable picnic in a tropical forest it would be difficult to imagine.

Perhaps the number of the Indians scared the jaguars away, for none appeared.

Yet the day was not to end without an adventure.

Darkness in this country follows the short twilight so speedily, that Burly Bill did well to get clear of the forest's gloom while the sun was still well above the horizon.

He trusted to the compass and his own good sense as a forester to come out close to the spot where he had left the boat. But he was deceived. He struck the river a good mile and a half above the place where the steamer lay at anchor and the raft aground on the shoals.

Lower and lower sank the sun. The ground was wet and marshy, and the 'gators very much in evidence indeed.

Now the tapirs—and droll pig-bodied creatures they look, though in South America nearly as big as donkeys—are of a very retiring disposition, but not really solitary animals as cheap books on natural history would have us believe. They frequent low woods, where their long snouts enable them to pull down the tender twigs and foliage on which, with roots, which they can speedily unearth, they manage to exist—yes, and to wax fat and happy.

But they are strict believers in the doctrine of cleanliness, and are never found very far from water. They bathe every night.

Just when the returning picnic was within about half a mile of the boat, Burly Bill carrying Peggy on his shoulder because the ground was damp, a terrible scrimmage suddenly took place a few yards round a backwater.

There was grunting, squeaking, the splashing of water, and cries of pain.

"Hurry on, boys; hurry on; two of you are enough! It's your show, lads."

The boys needed no second bidding, and no sooner had they opened out the curve than a strange sight met their gaze.

# CHAPTER VI—"NOT ONE SINGLE DROP OF BLOOD SHED"

A gigantic and horribly fierce alligator had seized upon a strong young tapir, and was trying to drag it into the water.

The poor creature had both its feet set well in front, and was resisting with all its might, while two other larger animals, probably the parents, were clawing the cayman desperately with their fore-feet.

But ill, indeed, would it have fared with all three had not our heroes appeared just in the nick of time.

For several more of these scaly and fearsome reptiles were hurrying to the scene of action.

Dick's first shot was a splendid one. It struck the offending cayman in the eye, and went crashing through his brain.

The brute gasped, the blood flowed freely, and as he fell on his side, turning up his yellow belly, the young tapir got free, and was hurried speedily away to the woods.

Volley after volley was poured in on the enraged 'gators, but the boys had to retreat as they fought. Had they not done so, my story would have stopped short just here.

It was not altogether the sun's parting rays that so encrimsoned the water, but the blood of those old-world caymans.

Three in all were killed in addition to the one first shot. So that it is no wonder the boys felt elated.

Beeboo had supper waiting and there was nothing talked about that evening except their strange adventures in the beautiful forest.

Probably no one could sleep more soundly than did our heroes and heroine that night.

Next day, and next, they went on shore again, and on the third a huge jaguar, who fancied he would like to dine off Brawn's shoulder, fell a victim to Dick Temple's unerring aim.

But the raft never stirred nor moved for a whole week.

Said Bill to Jake one morning, as he took his meerschaum from his mouth:

"I think, Jake, and w'at I thinks be's this like. There ain't ne'er a morsel o' good smokin' and on'y just lookin' at that fine and valuable pile o' timber. It strikes me conclusive like that something 'ad better be done."

"And what would you propose, Bill?" said Jake.

"Well, Jake, you're captain like, and my proposition is subject to your disposition as it were. But I'd lighten her, and lighten her till she floats; then tow her off, and build up the odd timbers again."

"Good! You have a better head than I have, Bill; and it's you that should have been skipper, not me."

Nothing was done that day, however, except making a few more attempts with the steamer at full speed to tow her off. She did shift and slue round a little, but that was all.

Next morning dawned as beautifully as any that had gone before it.

There were fleecy clouds, however, hurrying across the sky as if on business bent, and the blue between them was bluer than ever our young folks had seen it.

Dick Temple, with Roland and Peggy, had made up their minds to go on shore for another day while the work of dismantling the raft went on.

But a fierce south wind began to blow, driving heavy black clouds before it, and lashing the river into foam.

One of those terrible tropic storms was evidently on the cards, and come it did right soon.

The darkest blackness was away to the west, and here, though no thunder could be heard, the lightning was very vivid. It was evident that this was the vortex of the hurricane, for only a few drops of rain fell around the raft.

The picnic scheme was of course abandoned, and all waited anxiously enough for something to come.

That something did come in less than an hour—the descent of the mighty Amazon in flood. Its tributaries had no doubt been swollen by the awful rain and water-spouts, and poured into the great queen of rivers double their usual discharge.

A bore is a curling wave like a shore breaker that rushes down the smaller rivers, and is terribly destructive to boating or to shipping.

The Amazon, however, did not rise like this. It came rushing almost silently down in a broad tall wave that appeared to stretch right across it, from the forest-clad bank where the raft lay to the far-off green horizon in the north.

But Burly Bill was quite prepared for eventualities.

Steam had been got up, the vessel's bows were headed for up stream, and the hawser betwixt raft and boat tautened.

On and on rushed the huge wave. It towered above the raft, even when fifty yards away, in the most threatening manner, as if about to sweep all things to destruction.

But on its nearer approach it glided in under the raft, and steamer as well —like some huge submarine monster such as we read of in fairy books of the long-long-ago—glided in under them, and seemed to lift them sky-high.

"Go ahead at full speed!"

It was the sonorous voice of Burly Bill shouting to the engineer.

"Ay, ay, sir!" came the cheery reply.

The screw went round with a rush.

It churned up a wake of foaming water as the *Peggy* began to forge ahead, and next minute, driven along on the breeze, the monster raft began to follow and was soon out and away beyond danger from rock or shoal.

Then arose to heaven a prayer of thankfulness, and a cheer so loud and long that even the parrots and monkeys in the forest depths heard it, and yelled and chattered till they frightened both 'gators and jaguars.

Just two weeks after these adventures, the little *Peggy* was at anchor, and the great raft safely beached.

Burly Bill was left in charge with his white men and his Indians, with Dick Temple to act as supercargo, and Jake Solomons with Roland and Peggy, not to mention the dog, started off for Pará.

In due course, but after many discomforts, they arrived there, and Jake, after taking rooms in a hotel, hurried off to secure his despatches from the post-office.

"No letters!" cried Jake, as his big brown fist came down with a bang on the counter. "Why, I see the very documents I came for in the pigeon-hole behind you!"

The clerk, somewhat alarmed at the attitude of this tall Yankee backwoodsman, pulled them out and looked at them.

"They cannot be delivered," he said.

"And why?" thundered Jake, "Inasmuch as to wherefore, you greasy-faced little whipper-snapper!"

"Not sufficient postage."

Jake thrust one hand into a front pocket, and one behind him. Then on the counter he dashed down a bag of cash and a six-chambered revolver.

"I'm Jake Solomons," he said. "There before you lies peace or war. Hand over the letters, and you'll have the rhino. Refuse, and I guess and calculate I'll blow the whole top of your head off."

The clerk preferred peace, and Jake strode away triumphant.

When he returned to the hotel and told the boys the story, they laughed heartily. In their eyes, Jake was more a hero than ever.

"Ah!" said the giant quietly, "there's nothing brings these long-shore chaps sooner to their senses than letting 'em have a squint down the barrel of a six-shooter."

The letters were all from Mr. St. Clair, and had been lying at the post-office for over a week. They all related to business, to the sale of the timber and the other commodities, the best markets, and so on and so forth, with hints as to the gold-mine.

But the last one was much more bulky than the others, and so soon as he had glanced at the first lines, Jake lit his meerschaum, then threw himself back in his rocker to quietly discuss it.

It was a plain, outspoken letter, such as one man of the world writes to another. Here is one extract:—

*Our business is increasing at a rapid rate, Jake Solomon. I have too much to do and so have you; therefore, although I did not think it necessary to inform you before, I have been in communication with my brother John, and he is sending me out a shrewd, splendid man of business. He will have arrived before your return.*

*I can trust John thoroughly, and this Don Pedro Salvador, over and above his excellent business capabilities, can talk Spanish, French, and Portuguese.*

*I do not quite like the name, Jake, so he must be content to be called plain Mr. Peter.*

---

About the very time that Jake Solomons was reading this letter, there sat close to the sky-light of an outward-bound steamer at Liverpool, two men holding low but earnest conversation. Their faces were partly obscured, for it was night, and the only light a glimmer from the ship's lamp.

Steam was up and roaring through the pipes.

A casual observer might have noted that one was a slim, swarthy, but wiry, smart-looking man of about thirty. His companion was a man considerably over forty.

"I shall go now," said the latter. "You have my instructions, and I believe I can trust you."

"Have I not already given you reason to?" was the rejoinder. "At the risk of penal servitude did I not steal my employer's keys, break into his room at night, and copy that will for you? It was but a copy of a copy, it is true, and I could not discover the original, else the quickest and simplest plan would have been—fire:"

"True, you did so, but"—the older man laughed lightly—"you were well paid for the duty you performed."

"Duty, eh?" sneered the other. "Well," he added, "thank God nothing has been discovered. My employer has bidden me an almost affectionate farewell, and given me excellent certificates."

The other started up as a loud voice hailed the deck:

"Any more for the shore!"

"I am going now," he said. "Good-bye, old man, and remember my last words: not one single drop of blood shed!"

"I understand, and will obey to the letter. Obedience pays."

"True; and you shall find it so. Good-bye!"

"*A Dios!*" said the other.

The last bell was struck, and the gangway was hauled on shore.

The great ship *Benedict* was that night rolling and tossing about on the waves of the Irish Channel.

————————

Jake Solomons acquainted Roland and Peggy with the contents of this last letter, and greatly did the latter wonder what the new overseer would be like, and if she should love him or not.

For Peggy had a soft little heart of her own, and was always prepared to be friendly with anyone who, according to her idea, was nice.

Jake took his charges all round the city next day and showed them the sights of what is now one of the most beautiful towns in South America.

The gardens, the fountains, the churches and palaces, the flowers and fruit, and feathery palm-trees, all things indeed spoke of delightfulness, and calm, and peace.

And far beyond and behind all this was the boundless forest primeval.

This was not their last drive through the city, and this good fellow Jake, though his business took him from home most of the day, delighted to take the children to every place of amusement he could think of. But despite all this, these children of the forest wilds began to long for home, and very much rejoiced were they when one evening, after dinner, Jake told them they should start on the morrow for Bona Vista, near to which town the little steamer lay, and so up the great river and home.

Jake had done all his business, and done it satisfactorily, and could return to the old plantation and Burnley Hall with a light and cheerful heart.

He had even sold the mine, although it was not to be worked for some time to come.

# CHAPTER VII—"A COLD HAND SEEMED TO CLUTCH HER HEART"

Many months passed away pleasantly and happily enough on the old plantation. The children—Roland, by the way, would hardly have liked to be called a child now—were, of course, under the able tuition of Mr. Simons, but in addition Peggy had a governess, imported directly from Pará.

This was a dark-eyed Spanish girl, very piquant and pretty, who talked French well, and played on both the guitar and piano.

Tom St. Clair had not only his boy's welfare, but his niece's, or adopted daughter's, also at heart.

It would be some years yet before she arrived at the age of sweet seventeen, but when she did, her uncle determined to sell off or realize on his plantation, his goods and chattels, and sail across the seas once more to dear old Cornwall and the real Burnley Hall.

He looked forward to that time as the weary worker in stuffy towns or cities does to a summer holiday.

There is excitement enough in money-making, it is like an exhilarating game of billiards or whist, but it is apt to become tiresome.

And Tom St. Clair was often overtired and weary. He was always glad when he reached home at night to his rocking-chair and a good dinner, after toiling all day in the recently-started india-rubber-forest works.

But Mr. Peter took a vast deal of labour off his hands.

Mr. Peter, or Don Pedro, ingratiated himself with nearly everyone from the first, and seemed to take to the work as if to the manner born.

There were three individuals, however, who could not like him, strange to say; these were Peggy herself, Benee the Indian who had guided them through the forest when lost, and who had remained on the estate ever since, while the third was Brawn, the Irish wolf-hound.

The dog showed his teeth if Peter tried even to caress him.

Both Roland and Dick—the latter was a very frequent visitor—got on very well with Peter—trusted him thoroughly.

"How is it, Benee," said Roland one day to the Indian, "that you do not love Don Pedro?"

Benee spat on the ground and stamped his foot.

"I watch he eye," the semi-savage replied. "He one very bad man. Some day you know plenty moochee foh true."

"Well," said Tom one evening as he and his wife sat alone in the verandah together, "I do long to get back to England. I am tired, dear wife— my heart is weak why should we remain here over two years more? We are wealthy enough, and I promise myself and you, dear, many long years of health and happiness yet in the old country."

He paused and smoked a little; then, after watching for a few moments the fireflies that flitted from bush to bush, he stretched his left arm out and rested his hand on his wife's lap.

Some impulse seized her. She took it and pressed it to her lips. But a tear trickled down her cheek as she did so.

Lovers still this couple were, though nearly twenty years had elapsed since he led her, a bonnie, buxom, blushing lassie, to the altar.

But now in a sweet, low, but somewhat sad voice he sang a verse of that dear old song—"We have lived and loved together":—

"We have lived and loved together

Through many changing years,

We have shared each other's gladness

And dried each other's tears.

I have never known a sorrow

That was long unsoothed by thee,

For thy smile can make a summer

Where darkness else would be.

Mrs. St. Clair would never forget that evening on the star-lit lawn, nor the flitting, little fire-insects, nor her husband's voice.

––––––––––

Is it not just when we expect it least that sorrow sometimes falls suddenly upon us, hiding or eclipsing all our promised happiness and joy?

I have now to write a pitiful part of my too true story, but it must be done.

Next evening St. Clair rode home an hour earlier.

He complained of feeling more tired than usual, and said he would lie down on the drawing-room sofa until dinner was ready.

Peggy went singing along the hall to call him at the appointed time.

She went singing into the room.

"Pa, dear," she cried merrily; "Uncle-pa, dinner is all beautifully ready!"

"Come, Unky-pa. How sound you sleep!"

Then a terror crept up from the earth, as it were, and a cold hand seemed to clutch her heart.

She ran out of the room.

"Oh, Auntie-ma!" she cried, "come, come quickly, pa won't wake, nor speak!"

Heigho! the summons had come, and dear "Uncle-pa" would never, never wake again.

This is a short chapter, but it is too sad to continue.

So falls the curtain on the first act of this life-drama.

# CHAPTER VIII—FIERCELY AND WILDLY BOTH SIDES FOUGHT

The gloomy event related in last chapter must not be allowed to cast a damper over our story.

Of course death is always and everywhere hovering near, but why should boys like you and me, reader, permit that truth to cloud our days or stand between us and happiness?

Two years, then, have elapsed since poor, brave Tom St. Clair's death.

He is buried near the edge of the forest in a beautiful enclosure where rare shrubs grow, and where flowers trail and climb far more beautiful than any we ever see in England.

At first Mrs. St. Clair had determined to sell all off and go back to the old country, but her overseer Jake Solomons and Mr. Peter persuaded her not to, or it seemed that it was their advice which kept her from carrying out her first intentions. But she had another reason, she found she could not leave that lonesome grave yet awhile.

So the years passed on.

The estate continued to thrive.

Roland was now a handsome young fellow in his eighteenth year, and Peggy, now beautiful beyond compare, was nearly fifteen.

Dick Temple, the bold and reckless huntsman and horseman, was quieter now in his attentions towards her. She was no longer the child that he could lift on to his broad young shoulders and carry, neighing and galloping like a frightened colt, round and round the lawn.

And Roland felt himself a man. He was more sober and sedate, and had taken over all his father's work and his father's responsibilities. But for all that, lightly enough lay the burden on his heart.

For he had youth on his side, and

"In the lexicon of youth which fate reserves

For a bright manhood there is no such word

As fail".

———————

I do not, however, wish to be misunderstood. It must not be supposed that Roland had no difficulties to contend with, that all his business life was as fair and serene as a bright summer's day. On the contrary, he had many losses owing to the fluctuations of the markets and the failures of great firms, owing to fearful storms, and more than once owing to strikes or revolts among his Indians in the great india-rubber forest.

But Roland was light-hearted and young, and difficulties in life, I have often said, are just like nine-pins, they are put up to be bowled over.

Besides, be it remembered that if it were all plain sailing with us in this world we should not be able to appreciate how really happy our lives are. The sky is always bluest 'twixt the darkest clouds.

On the whole, Roland, who took stock, and, with honest Bill and Jake Solomons, went over the books every quarter, had but little reason to complain. This stock-taking consumed most of their spare time for the greater part of a week, and when it was finished Roland invariably gave a dinner-party, at which I need hardly say his dear friend Dick Temple was present. And this was always the happiest of happy nights to Dick, because the girl he loved more than all things on earth put together was here, and looked so innocent and beautiful in her simple dresses of white and blue.

There was no such thing as flirtation here, but Dick was fully and completely in earnest when he told himself that if he lived till he was three- or four-and-twenty he would ask Peggy to be his wife.

Ah! there is many a slip 'twixt the cup and the lip.

Dick, I might, could, would, or should have told you before, lived with a bachelor uncle, who, being rather old and infirm, seldom came out. He had good earnest men under him, however, as overseers, and his plantations were thriving, especially that in which tobacco was cultivated.

The old man was exceedingly fond of Dick, and Dick would be his heir.

Probably it was for his uncle's sake that Dick stayed in the country—and of course for Peggy's and Roland's—for, despite its grand field for sport and adventure, the lad had a strange longing to go to England and play cricket or football.

He had been born in Britain just as Roland was, and had visited his childhood's home more than once during his short life.

Now just about this time Don Pedro, or Mr. Peter as all called him, had asked for and obtained a holiday. He was going to Pará for a change, he said, and to meet a friend from England.

That he did meet a friend from England there was little doubt, but their interview was a very short one. Where he spent the rest of his time was best known to himself.

In three months or a little less he turned up smiling again, and most effusive.

About a fortnight after his arrival he came to Jake one morning pretty early.

Jake was preparing to start on horseback for the great forest.

"I'm on the horns of a dilemma, Mr. Solomons," he said, laughing his best laugh. "During the night about twenty Bolivian Indians have encamped near to the forest. They ask for work on the india-rubber trees. They are well armed, and all sturdy warriors. They look as if fighting was more in their line than honest labour."

"Well, Mr. Peter, what is their excuse for being here anyhow?"

"They are bound for the sea-shore at the mouths of the river, and want to earn a few dollars to help them on."

"Well, where is the other horn of the dilemma?"

"Oh! if I give them work they may corrupt our fellows."

"Then, Mr. Peter, I'd give the whole blessed lot the boot and the sack."

"Ah! now, Mr. Solomons, you've got to the other horn. These savages, for they are little else, are revengeful."

"We're not afraid."

"No, we needn't be were they to make war openly, but they are sly, and as dangerous as sly. They would in all probability burn us down some dark night."

Jake mused for a minute. Then he said abruptly:

"Let the poor devils earn a few dollars, Mr. Peter, if they are stony-broke, and then send them on their way rejoicing."

"That's what I say, too," said Burly Bill, who had just come up. "I've been over yonder in the starlight. They look deuced uncouth and nasty. So does a bull-dog, Jake, but is there a softer-hearted, more kindly dog in all creation?"

So that very day the Indians set to work with the other squads.

The labour connected with the collecting of india-rubber is by no means very hard, but it requires a little skill, and is irksome to those not used to such toil.

But labour is scarce and Indians are often lazy, so on the whole Jake was not sorry to have the new hands, or "serinqueiros" as they are called.

The india-rubber trees are indigenous and grow in greatest profusion on that great tributary of the Amazon called the Madeira. But when poor Tom St. Clair came to the country he had an eye to business. He knew that india-rubber would always command a good market, and so he visited the distant forests, studied the growth and culture of the trees as conducted by Nature, and ventured to believe that he could improve upon her methods.

He was successful, and it was not a great many years before he had a splendid plantation of young trees in his forest, to say nothing of the older ones that had stood the brunt of many a wild tropical storm.

It will do no harm if I briefly describe the method of obtaining the india-rubber. Tiny pots of tin, holding about half a pint, are hung under an incision in the bark of the tree, and these are filled and emptied every day, the contents being delivered by the Indian labourers at the house or hut of an under-overseer.

The sap is all emptied into larger utensils, and a large smoking fire, made of the nuts of a curious kind of palm called the Motokoo, being built, the operators dip wooden shovels into the sap, twirling these round quickly and holding them in the smoke. Coagulation takes place very quickly. Again the shovel is dipped in the sap, and the same process is repeated until the coagulated rubber is about two inches thick, when it is cooled, cut, or sliced off, and is ready for the distant market.

Now, from the very day of their arrival, there was no love lost between the old and steady hands and this new band of independent and flighty ones.

The latter were willing enough to slice the bark and to hang up their pannikins, and they would even empty them when filled, and condescend to carry their contents to the preparing-house. But they were lazy in the extreme at gathering the nuts, and positively refused to smoke the sap and coagulate it.

It made them weep, they explained, and it was much more comfortable to lie and wait for the sap while they smoked and talked in their own strange language.

After a few days the permanent hands refused to work at the same trees, or even in the same part of the estrados or roads that led through the plantation of rubber-trees.

A storm was brewing, that was evident. Nor was it very long before it burst.

All unconscious that anything was wrong, Peggy, with Brawn, was romping about one day enjoying the busy scene, Peggy often entering into conversation with some of her old favourites, when one of the strange Indians, returning from the tub with an empty tin, happened to tread on Brawn's tail.

The dog snarled, but made no attempt to bite. Afraid, however, that he would spring upon the fellow, Peggy threw herself on the ground, encircling her arms around Brawn's shoulders, and it was she who received the blow that was meant for the dog.

It cut her across the arm, and she fainted with pain.

Brawn sprang at once upon his man and brought him down.

*"BRAWN SPRANG AT ONCE UPON HIS MAN"*

He shook the wretch as if he had been but a rat, and blood flowed freely.

Burly Bill was not far off, and just as the great hound had all but fixed the savage by the windpipe, which he would undoubtedly have torn out, Bill pulled him off by the collar and pacified him.

The blood-stained Indian started to his legs to make good his retreat, but as his back was turned in flight, Bill rushed after him and dealt him a kick that laid him prone on his face.

This was the signal for a general mêlée, and a terrible one it was!

Bill got Peggy pulled to one side, and gave her in charge to Dick, who had come thundering across on his huge horse towards the scene of conflict.

Under the shelter of a spreading tree Dick lifted his precious charge. But she speedily revived when he laid her flat on the ground. She smiled feebly and held out her hand, which Dick took and kissed, the tears positively trickling over his cheeks.

Perhaps it was a kind of boyish impulse that caused him to say what he now said:

"Oh, Peggy, my darling, how I love you! Whereever you are, dear, wherever I am—oh, always think of me a little!"

That was all.

A faint colour suffused Peggy's cheek for just a moment. Then she sat up, and the noble hound anxiously licked her face.

But she had made no reply.

Meanwhile the mêlée went merrily on, as a Donnybrook Irishman might remark.

Fiercely and wildly both sides fought, using as weapons whatsoever came handiest.

But soon the savages were beaten and discomfited with, sad to tell, the loss of one life—that of a savage.

Not only Jake himself, but Roland and Mr. Peter were now on the scene of the recent conflict. Close to Peter's side, watching every movement of his lips and eyes, stood Benee, the Indian who had saved the children.

Several times Peter looked as if he felt uneasy, and once he turned towards Benee as if about to speak.

He said nothing, and the man continued his watchful scrutiny.

After consulting for a short time together, Jake and Roland, with Burly Bill, determined to hold a court of inquiry on the spot.

But, strange to say, Peter kept aloof. He continued to walk to and fro, and Benee still hung in his rear. But this ex-savage was soon called upon to act as interpreter if his services should be needed, which they presently were.

Every one of the civilized Indians had the same story to tell of the laziness and insolence of the Bolivians, and now Jake ordered the chief of the other party to come forward.

They sulked for a short time.

But Jake drew his pistols, and, one in each hand, stepped out and ordered all to the front.

They made no verbal response to the questions put to them through Benee. Their only reply was scowling.

"Well, Mr. St. Clair," said Jake, "my advice is to pay these rascals and send them off."

"Good!" said Roland. "I have money."

The chief was ordered to draw nearer, and the dollars were counted into his claw-like fist.

The fellow drew up his men in a line and gave to each his pay, reserving his own.

Then at a signal, given by the chief, there was raised a terrible war-whoop and howl.

The chief spat on his dollars and dashed them into a neighbouring pool. Every man did the same.

Roland was looking curiously on. He was wondering what would happen next.

He had not very long to wait, for with his foot the chief turned the dead man on his back, and the blood from his death-stab poured out afresh.

He dipped his palm in the red stream and held it up on high. His men followed his example.

Then all turned to the sun, and in one voice uttered just one word, which, being interpreted by Benee, was understood to mean—REVENGE!

They licked the blood from their hands, and, turning round, marched in silence and in single file out and away from the forest and were seen no more.

# CHAPTER IX—THAT TREE IN THE FOREST GLADE

The things, the happenings, I have now to tell you of in this chapter form the turning-point in our story.

Weeks passed by after the departure of that mysterious band of savages, and things went on in the same old groove on the plantation.

Whence the savages had come, or whither they had gone, none could tell. But all were relieved at their exit, dramatic and threatening though it had been.

The hands were all very busy now everywhere, and one day, it being the quarter's end, after taking stock Roland gave his usual dinner-party, and a ball to his natives. These were all dressed out as gaily as gaily could be. The ladies wore the most tawdry of finery, most of which they had bought, or rather had had brought them by their brothers and lovers from Pará, and nothing but the most pronounced evening dress did any "lady of colour" deign to wear.

Why should they not ape the quality, and "poh deah Miss Peggy".

Peggy was very happy that evening, and so I need hardly say was Dick Temple. Though he never had dared to speak of love again, no one could have looked at those dark daring eyes of his and said it was not there.

It must have been about eleven by the clock and a bright moonlight night when Dick started to ride home. He knew the track well, he said, and could not be prevailed upon to stay all night. Besides, his uncle expected him.

The dinner and ball given to the plantation hands had commenced at sunset, or six o'clock, and after singing hymns—a queer finish to a most hilarious dance—all retired, and by twelve of the clock not a sound was to be heard over all the plantation save now and then the mournful cry of the shriek-owl or a plash in the river, showing that the 'gators preferred a moonshiny night to daylight itself.

The night wore on, one o'clock, two o'clock chimed from the turret on Burnley Hall, and soon after this, had anyone been in the vicinity he would have seen a tall figure, wrapped in cloak and hood, steal away from the house adown the walks that led from the flowery lawns. The face was quite hidden, but several times the figure paused, as if to listen and glance around, then hurried on once more, and finally disappeared in the direction of the forest.

Peggy's bedroom was probably the most tastefully-arranged and daintily-draped in the house, and when she lay down to-night and fell gently asleep, very sweet indeed were the dreams that visited her pillow. The room was on a level with the river lawn, on to which it opened by a French or casement window. Three o'clock!

The moon shone on the bed, and even on the girl's face, but did not awaken her.

A few minutes after this, and the casement window was quietly opened, and the same cloaked figure, which stole away from the mansion an hour before, softly entered.

It stood for more than half a minute erect and listening, then, bending low beside the bed, listened a moment there.

Did no spectral dream cross the sleeping girl's vision to warn her of the dreadful fate in store for her?

Had she shrieked even now, assistance would have been speedily forthcoming, and she might have been saved!

But she quietly slumbered on.

Then the dark figure retreated as it had come, and presently another and more terrible took its place—a burly savage carrying a blanket or rug.

First the girl's clothing and shoes, her watch and all her trinkets, were gathered up and handed to someone on the lawn.

Then the savage, approaching the bed with stealthy footsteps, at once enveloped poor Peggy in the rug and bore her off.

For a moment she uttered a muffled moan or two, like a nightmare scream, then all was still as the grave.

---

"Missie Peggy! Missie Peggy," cried Beeboo next morning at eight as she entered the room. "What for you sleep so long? Ah!" she added sympathizingly, still holding the door-knob in her hand. "Ah! but den the poh chile very tired. Dance plenty mooch las' night, and—"

She stopped suddenly.

Something unusual in the appearance of the bed attire attracted her attention and she speedily rushed towards it.

She gave vent at once to a loud yell, and Roland himself, who was passing near, ran in immediately.

He stood like one in a state of catalepsy, with his eyes fixed on the empty bed. But he recovered shortly.

"Oh, this is a fearful day!" he cried, and hastened out to acquaint Jake and Bill, both of whom, as well as Mr. Peter, slept in the east wing of the mansion.

He ran from door to door knocking very loud and shouting: "Awake, awake, Peggy has gone! She has been kidnapped, and the accursed savages have had their revenge!"

In their pyjamas only, Jake and Bill appeared, and after a while Mr. Peter, fully dressed.

He looked sleepy.

"I had too much wine last night," he said, with a yawn, "and slept very heavily all night. But what is the matter?"

He was quietly and quickly informed.

"This is indeed a fearful blow, but surely we can trace the scoundrels!"

"Boys, hurry through with your breakfast," said Roland. "Jake, I will be back in a few minutes."

He whistled shrilly and Brawn came rushing to his side.

"Follow me, Brawn."

His object was to find out in which direction the savages had gone.

Had Brawn been a blood-hound he could soon have picked up the scent.

As it was, however, his keen eyes discovered the trail on the lawn, and led him to the gate. He howled impatiently to have it opened, then bounded out and away towards the forest in a westerly and southerly direction, which, if pursued far enough, would lead towards Bolivia, along the wild rocky banks of the Madeira River.

It was a whole hour before Brawn returned. He carried something in his mouth. He soon found his master, and laid the something gently down at his feet, stretching himself—grief-stricken—beside it.

It was one of Peggy's boots, with a white silk stocking in it, drenched in blood.

The white men and Indians were now fully aroused, and, leaving Jake in charge of the estate, Roland picked out thirty of the best men, armed them with guns, and placed them under the command of Burly Bill. Then they started off in silence, Roland and Burly mounted, the armed whites and Indians on foot.

Brawn went galloping on in front in a very excited manner, often returning and barking wildly at the horses as if to hurry them on.

Throughout that forenoon they journeyed by the trail, which was now distinct enough, and led through the jungle and forest.

They came out on to a clearing about one o'clock. Here was water in abundance, and as they were all thoroughly exhausted, they threw themselves down by the spring to quench their thirst and rest.

Bill made haste now to deal out the provisions, and after an hour, during which time most of them slept, they resumed their journey.

A mile or two farther on they came to a sight which almost froze their blood.

In the middle of a clearing or glade stood a great tree. It was hollowed out at one side, and against this was still a heap of half-charred wood, evidently the remains of a fierce fire, though every ember had died black out.

Here was poor Peggy's other shoe. That too was bloody.

And here was a pool of coagulated blood, with huge rhinoceros beetles busy at their work of excavation. Portions or rags of dress also!

It was truly an awful sight!

Roland reined up his horse, and placed his right hand over his eyes.

"Bill," he managed to articulate, "can you have the branches removed, and let us know the fearful worst?"

Burly Bill gave the order, and the Indians tossed the half-burned wood aside.

Then they pulled out bone after bone of limbs, of arms, of ribs. But all were charred almost into cinders!

Roland now seemed to rise to the occasion.

He held his right arm on high.

"Bill," he cried; "here, under the blazing sun and above the remains, the dust of my dead sister, I register a vow to follow up these fiends to their distant homes, if Providence shall but lead us aright, and to slay and burn every wretch who has aided or abetted this terrible deed!"

"I too register that vow," said Bill solemnly.

"And I, and I!" shouted the white men, and even the Indians.

They went on again once more, after burying the charred bones and dust.

But the trail took them to a ford, and beyond the stream there was not the imprint of even a single footstep.

The retiring savages must either have doubled back on their tracks or waded for miles up or down the rocky stream before landing.

Nothing more could be done to-day, for the sun was already declining, and they must find their way out of the gloom of the forest before darkness. So the return journey was made, and just as the sun's red beams were crimsoning the waters of the western river, they arrived once more at the plantation and Burnley Hall.

The first to meet them was Peter himself. He seemed all anxiety.

"What have you found?" he gasped.

It was a moment or two before Roland could reply.

"Only the charred remains of my poor sister!" he said at last, then compressed his mouth in an effort to keep back the tears.

The Indian who took so lively an interest in Mr. Peter was not far away, and was watching his man as usual.

None noticed, save Benee himself, that Mr. Peter heaved something very like a sigh of relief as Roland's words fell on his ears.

Burnley Hall was now indeed a castle of gloom; but although poor Mrs. St. Clair was greatly cast down, the eager way in which Roland and Dick were making their preparations to follow up the savage Indians, even to the confines or interior, if necessary, of their own domains, gave her hope.

Luckily they had already found a clue to their whereabouts, for one of the civilized Bolivians knew that very chief, and indeed had come from the same far-off country. He described the people as a race of implacable savages and cannibals, into whose territory no white man had ever ventured and returned alive.

Were they a large tribe? No, not large, not over three or four thousand, counting women and children. Their arms? These were spears and broad two-bladed knives, with great slings, from which they could hurl large stones and pieces of flint with unerring accuracy, and bows and arrows. And no number of white men could stand against these unless they sheltered themselves in trenches or behind rocks and trees.

This ex-cannibal told them also that the land of this terrible tribe abounded in mineral wealth, in silver ore and even in gold.

For this information Roland cared little; all he wished to do was to avenge poor Peggy's death. If his men, after the fighting, chose to lay out claims he would permit a certain number of them to do so, their names to be drawn by ballot. The rest must accompany the expedition back.

Dick's uncle needed but little persuasion to give forty white men, fully armed and equipped, to swell Roland's little army of sixty whites. Besides these, they would have with them carriers and ammunition-bearers—Indians from the plantations.

Dick was all life and fire. If they were successful, he himself, he said, would shoot the murderous chief, or stab him to the heart.

A brave show indeed did the little army make, when all mustered and drilled, and every man there was most enthusiastic, for all had loved poor lost Peggy.

"I shall remain at my post here, I suppose," said Mr. Peter.

"If I do not alter my mind I shall leave you and Jake, with Mr. Roberts, the tutor, to manage the estate in my absence," said Roland.

He did alter his mind, and, as the following will show, he had good occasion to do so.

One evening the strange Indian Benee, between whom and Peter there existed so much hatred, sought Roland out when alone.

"Can I speakee you, all quiet foh true?"

"Certainly, my good fellow. Come into my study. Now, what is it you would say?"

"Dat Don Pedro no true man! I tinkee much, and I tinkee dat."

"Well, I know you don't love each other, Benee; but can you give me any proofs of his villainy?"

"You letee me go to-night all myse'f alone to de bush. I tinkee I bring you someding strange. Some good news. Ha! it may be so!"

"I give you leave, and believe you to be a faithful fellow."

Benee seized his master's hand and bent down his head till his brow touched it.

Next moment he was gone.

Next morning he was missed.

"Your pretty Indian," said Mr. Peter, with an ill-concealed sneer, "is a traitor, then, after all, and a spy, and it was no doubt he who instigated the abduction and the murder, for the sake of revenge, of your poor little sister."

"That remains to be seen, Mr. Peter. If he, or anyone else on the plantation, is a traitor, he shall hang as high as Haman."

Peter cowered visibly, but smiled his agitation off.

And that same night about twelve, while Roland sat smoking on the lawn with Dick, all in the moonlight, everyone else having retired—smoking and talking of the happy past—suddenly the gate hinges creaked, and with a low growl Brawn sprang forward. But he returned almost immediately, wagging his tail and being caressed by Benee himself.

Silently stood the Indian before them, silently as a statue, but in his left hand he carried a small bundle bound up in grass. It was not his place to speak first, and both young men were a little startled at his sudden appearance.

"What, Benee! and back so soon from the forest?"

"Benee did run plenty quickee. Plenty jaguar want eat Benee, but no can catchee."

"Well?"

"I would speekee you bof boys in de room."

The two started up together.

Here was some mystery that must be unravelled.

# CHAPTER X—BENEE MAKES A STRANGE DISCOVERY

Benee followed them into Roland's quiet study, and placed his strange grass-girt bundle on a cane chair.

Roland gave him a goblet of wine-and-water, which he drank eagerly, for he was faint and tired.

"Now, let us hear quickly what you have to say, Benee."

The Indian came forward, and his words, though uttered with some vehemence, and accompanied by much gesticulation, were delivered in almost a whisper.

It would have been impossible for any eavesdropper in the hall to have heard.

"Wat I tellee you 'bout dat Peter?" he began.

"My good friend," said Roland, "Peter accuses you of being a spy and traitor."

"I killee he!"

"No, you will not; if Peter is guilty, I will see that justice overtakes him."

"Well, 'fore I go, sah, I speakee you and say I bringee you de good news."

"Tell us quickly!" said Dick in a state of great excitement.

"Dis, den, is de good news: Missie Peggy not dead! No, no!"

"Explain, Benee, and do not raise false hopes in our breasts."

"De cannibals make believe she murder; dat all is."

"But have we not found portions of her raiment, her blood-dripping stockings, and also her charred remains?"

"Listen, sah. Dese cannibals not fools. Dey beat you plenty of trail, so you can easily find de clearing where de fire was. Dey wis' you to go to dat tree to see de blood, de shoe, and all. But when you seekee de trail after, where is she? Tellee me dat. Missie Peggy no murder. No, no. She am carried away, far away, as one prisint to de queen ob de cannibals."

"What were the bones, my good Benee?"

Then Benee opened his strange bundle, and there fell on the floor the half-burned skull and jaws of a gigantic baboon.

"I find dat hid beside de tree. Ha, ha!"

"It is all clear now," said Roland. "My dear, faithful Benee," he continued, "can you guide us to the country of the cannibals? You will meet your reward, both here and hereafter."

"I not care. I lub Missie Peggy. Ah, she come backee once moh, foh true!"

And now Dick Temple, the impulsive, must step forward and seize Benee by the hand. "God bless you!" he said; and indeed it was all he could say.

When the Indian had gone, Roland and Dick drew closer together.

"The mystery," said the former, "seems to me, Dick, to be as dark and intricate as ever. I can understand the savages carrying poor Peggy away, but why the tricky deceit, the dropped shoe that poor, noble Brawn picked up, the pool of blood, the rent and torn garments, and the half-charred bones?"

"Well, I think I can see through that, Roland. I believe it was done to prevent your further pursuit; for, as Benee observes, the trail is left plainly enough for even a white man to see as far as the 'fire-tree' and on to the brook. But farther there is none."

"Well, granting all this; think you, Dick, that no one instigated them, probably even suggested the crime and the infernal deceit they have practised?"

"Now you are thinking of, if not actually accusing, Mr. Peter?"

"I am, Dick. I have had my suspicions of him ever since a month after he came. It was strange how Benee hated him from the beginning, to say nothing of Brawn, the dog, and our dear lost Peggy."

"Cheer up!" said Dick. "Give Peter a show, though things look dark against him."

"Yes," said Roland sternly, "and with us and our expedition he must and shall go. We can watch his every move, and if I find that he is a villain, may God have mercy on his soul! His body shall feed the eagles."

Dick Temple was a wild and reckless boy, it is true, and always first, if possible, in any adventure which included a spice of danger, but he had a good deal of common sense notwithstanding.

He mused a little, and rolled himself a fresh cigarette before he replied.

"Your Mr. Peter," he said, "may or may not be guilty of duplicity, though I do not see the *raison d'être* for any such conduct, and I confess to you that I look upon lynching as a wild kind of justice. At the same time I must again beg of you, Roland, to give the man a decent show."

"Here is my hand on that, Dick. He shall have justice, even should that just finish with his dangling at a rope's end."

The two shortly after this parted for the night, each going to his own room, but I do not think that either of them slept till long past midnight.

They were up in good time, however, for the bath, and felt invigorated and hungry after the dip.

They were not over-merry certainly, but Mrs. St. Clair was quite changed, and just a little hysterically hilarious. For as soon as he had tubbed, Roland had gone to her bedroom and broken the news to her which Benee had brought.

That same forenoon Dick and Roland rode out to the forest.

They could hear the boom and shriek and roar of the great buzz-saw long before they came near the white-men's quarters.

They saw Jake,—and busy enough he was too,—and told him that they had some reason to doubt the honesty or sincerity of Mr. Peter, and that they would take him along with them.

"Thank God!" said Jake most fervently. "I myself cannot trust a man whom a dog like Brawn and a savage like Benee have come to hate."

By themselves that day the young fellows completed their plans, and all would now be ready to advance in a week's time.

That same day, however, on parade and in presence of Mr. Peter, Roland made a little speech.

"We are going," he said, "my good fellows, on a very long and adventurous journey. Poor Miss Peggy is, as we all know" (this was surely a fib that would be forgiven) "dead and gone, but we mean to follow these savages up to their own country, and deal them such a blow as will paralyse them for years. Yellow Charlie yonder is himself one of their number, but he has proved himself faithful, and has offered to be our guide as soon as we enter unknown regions.

"I have," he added, "perfect faith in my white men, faith in Mr. Peter, whom I am taking with me—"

Peter took a step forward as if to speak, but Roland waved him back.

"And I know my working Indians will prove themselves good men and true.

"After saying this, it is hardly necessary to add that if anyone is found attempting to desert our column, even should it be Burly Bill himself" (Burly Bill laughed outright), "he will be shot down as we would shoot a puma or alligator."

There was a wild cheer after Roland stepped down from the balcony, and in this Mr. Peter seemed to join so heartily that Roland's heart smote him.

For perhaps, after all, he had been unkind in thought to this man.

Time alone would tell.

The boys determined to leave nothing to chance, but ammunition was of even more importance than food. They hoped to find water everywhere, and the biscuits carried, with the roots they should dig, would serve to keep the expedition alive and healthy, with the aid of their good guns.

Medicine was not forgotten, nor medical comforts.

For three whole days Roland trained fast-running Indians to pick up a trail. A man would be allowed to have three miles' start, and then, when he was quite invisible, those human sleuth-hounds would be let loose, and they never failed to bring back their prisoner after a time.

One man at least was much impressed by these trials of skill.

Just a week before the start, and late in the evening, Benee once more presented himself before our young heroes.

"I would speakee you!"

"Well, Benee, say what you please, but all have not yet retired. Dick, get out into the hall, and warn us if anyone approaches."

Dick jumped up, threw his cigarette away, and did as he was told.

"Thus I speakee you and say," said Benee. "You trustee I?"

"Assuredly!"

"Den you let me go?"

"How and where?"

"I go fast as de wind, fleeter dan de rain-squall, far ober de mountains ob Madeira, far froo' de wild, dark forest. I heed noting, I fear noting. No wil'

85

beas' makee Benee 'fraid. I follow de cannibals. I reach de country longee time 'foh you. I creepee like one snake to de hut ob poh deah Peggy. She no can fly wid me, but I 'sure her dat you come soon, in two moon p'laps, or free. I make de chile happy. Den I creep and glide away again all samee one black snake, and come back to find you. I go?"

Roland took the man's hand. Savage though he was, there was kindness and there was undoubted sincerity in those dark, expressive eyes, and our hero at once gave the permission asked.

"But," he said, "the way is long and dangerous, my good Benee, so here I give you two long-range six-shooters, a repeating-rifle, and a box of cartridges. May God speed your journey, and bring you safely back with news that shall inspire our hearts! Go!"

Benee glided away as silently as he had come, and next morning his place was found empty. But would their trust in this man reap its reward, or— awful doubt—was Benee false?

Next night but one something very strange happened.

All was silent in and around Burnley Hall, and the silvery tones of the great tower clock had chimed the hour of three, when the window of Mr. Peter's room was silently opened, and out into the moonlight glided the man himself.

He carried in his hand a heavy grip-sack, and commenced at once taking the path that led downwards to the river.

Here lay the dinghy boat drawn up on the beach. She was secured with padlock and chain, but all Roland's officers carried keys.

It was about a quarter of a mile to the river-side, and Peter was proceeding at a fairly rapid rate, considering the weight of his grip-sack.

He had a habit of talking to himself. He was doing so now.

"I have only to drop well down the river and intercept a steamer. It is this very day they pass, and—"

Two figures suddenly glided from the bush and stood before him.

One sprang up behind, whom he could not see.

"Good-morning, Mr. Peter! Going for a walk early, aren't you? It's going to turn out a delightful day, I think."

They were white men.

"Here!" cried Peter, "advance but one step, or dare to impede my progress, and you are both dead men! I am a good shot, and happen, as you see, to have the draw on you."

Next moment his right arm was seized from behind, the men in front ducked, and the first shot went off in the air.

"Here, none o' that, guv'nor!" said a set, determined voice.

The revolver was wrenched from his grasp, and he found himself on his back in the pathway.

"It is murder you'd be after! Eh?"

"Not so, my good fellow," said Peter. "I will explain."

"Explain, then."

"My duties are ended with Mr. Roland St. Clair. He owes me one month's wages. I have forfeited that and given warning, and am going. That is all."

"You are going, are you? Well, we shall see about that."

"Yes, you may, and now let me pass on my peaceful way."

"He! he! he! But tell us, Mr. Peter, why this speedy departure? Hast aught upon thy conscience, or hast got a conscience?"

Peter had risen to his feet.

"Merely this. I claim the privilege of every working man, that of giving leave. I am not strong, and I dread the long journey Mr. St. Clair and his little band are to take."

"But," said the other, "you came in such a questionable shape, and we were here to watch for stragglers, not of course thinking for a moment, Mr. Peter, that your French window would be opened, and that you yourself would attempt to take French leave.

"Now you really must get back to your bedroom, guv'nor, and see Mr. St. Clair in the morning. My mates will do sentry-go at your window, and I shall be by your door in case you need anything. It is a mere matter of form, Mr. Peter, but of course we have to obey orders. Got ere a drop of brandy in your flask?"

Peter quickly produced quite a large bottle. He drank heavily himself first, and then passed it round.

But the men took but little, and Mr. Peter, half-intoxicated, allowed himself to be conducted to bed.

When these sentries gave in their report next morning to Roland, Mr. Peter did not rise a deal in the young fellow's estimation.

"It only proves one thing," he said to Dick. "If Peter is so anxious to give us the slip, we must watch him well until we are far on the road towards the cannibals' land."

"That's so," returned Dick Temple.

Not a word was said to Peter regarding his attempted flight when he sat down to breakfast with the boys, and naturally enough he believed it had not been reported. Indeed he had some hazy remembrance of having offered the sentries a bribe to keep dark.

Mr. Peter ate very sparingly, and looked sadly fishy about the eyes.

But he made no more attempts to escape just then.

# CHAPTER XI—ALL ALONE IN THE WILDERNESS

That Benee was a good man and true we have little reason to doubt, up to the present time at all events.

Yet Dick Temple was, curiously enough, loth to believe that Mr. Peter was other than a friend. And nothing yet had been proved against him.

"Is it not natural enough," said he to Roland, "that he should funk—to put it in fine English—the terrible expedition you and I are about to embark upon? And knowing that you have commanded him to accompany us would, in my opinion, be sufficient to account for his attempt to escape and drop down the river to Pará, and so home to his own country. Roland, I repeat, we must give the man a show."

"True," said Roland, "and poor Benee is having his show. Time alone can prove who the traitor is. If it be Benee he will not return. On the contrary, he will join the savage captors of poor Peggy, and do all in his power to frustrate our schemes."

No more was said.

But the preparations were soon almost completed, and in a day or two after this, farewells being said, the brave little army began by forced marches to find its way across country and through dense forests and damp marshes, and over rocks and plains, to the Madeira river, high above its junction with the great Amazon.

———————

Meanwhile let us follow the lonely Indian in his terrible journey to the distant and unexplored lands of Bolivia.

Like all true savages, he despised the ordinary routes of traffic or trade;

his track must be a bee-line, guiding himself by the sun by day, but more particularly by the stars by night.

Benee knew the difference betwixt stars and planets. The latter were always shifting, but certain stars—most to him were like lighthouses to mariners who are approaching land—shone over the country of the cannibals, and he could tell from their very altitude how much progress he was making night after night.

So lonesome, so long, was his thrice dreary journey, that had it been undertaken by a white man, in all probability he would soon have been a raving maniac.

But Benee had all the cunning, all the daring, and all the wisdom of a true savage, and for weeks he felt a proud exhilaration, a glorious sense of freedom and happiness, at being once more his own master, no work to do, and hope ever pointing him onwards to his goal.

What was that goal? it may well be asked. Was Benee disinterested? Did he really feel love for the white man and the white man's children? Can aught save selfishness dwell in the breast of a savage? In brief, was it he who had been the spy, he who was the guilty man; or was it Peter who was the villain? Look at it in any light we please, one thing is certain, this strange Indian was making his way back to his own country and to his own friends, and Indians are surely not less fond of each other than are the wild beasts who herd together in the forest, on the mountain-side, or on the ice in the far-off land of the frozen north. And well we know that these creatures will die for each other.

If there was a mystery about Peter, there was something approaching to one about Benee also.

But then it must be remembered that since his residence on the St. Clair plantation, Benee had been taught the truths of that glorious religion of ours, the religion of love that smoothes the rugged paths of life for us, that gives a silver lining to every cloud of grief and sorrow, and gilds even the dark portals of death itself.

Benee believed even as little children do. And little Peggy in her quiet moods used to tell him the story of life by redemption in her almost infantile way.

For all that, it is hard and difficult to vanquish old superstitions, and this man was only a savage at heart after all, though, nevertheless, there seemed to be much good in his rough, rude nature, and you may ofttimes see the sweetest and most lovely little flowers growing on the blackest and ruggedest of rocks.

Well, this journey of Benee's was certainly no sinecure. Apart even from all the dangers attached to it, from wild beasts and wilder men, it was one that would have tried the hardest constitution, if only for the simple reason that it was all a series of forced marches.

There was something in him that was hurrying him on and encouraging him to greater and greater exertions every hour. His daily record depended to a great extent on the kind of country he had to negotiate. He began with forty miles, but after a time, when he grew harder, he increased this to fifty and often to sixty. It was at times difficult for him to force his way through deep, dark forest and jungle, along the winding wild-beast tracks, past the beasts themselves, who hid in trees ready to spring had he paused but a second; through marshes and bogs, with here and there a reedy lake, on which aquatic birds of brightest colours slept as they floated in the sunshine, but among the long reeds of which lay the ever-watchful and awful cayman.

In such places as these, I think Benee owed his safety to his utter fearlessness and sang-froid, and to the speed at which he travelled.

It was not a walk by any means, but a strange kind of swinging trot. Such a gait may still be seen in far-off outlying districts of the Scottish Highlands, where it is adopted by postal "runners", who consider it not only faster but less tiresome than walking.

For the first hundred miles, or more, the lonely traveller found himself in a comparatively civilized country. This was not very much to his liking, and as a rule he endeavoured to give towns and villages, and even rubber forests, where Indians worked under white men overseers, a wide berth.

Yet sometimes, hidden in a tree, he would watch the work going on; watch the men walking hither and thither with their pannikins, or deftly whirling the shovels they had dipped in the sap-tub and holding them in the dark smoke of the palm-tree nuts, or he would listen to their songs. But it was with no feeling of envy; it was quite the reverse.

For Benee was free! Oh what a halo of happiness and glory surrounds that one little word "Free"!

Then this lonely wanderer would hug himself, as it were, and, dropping down from his perch, start off once more at his swinging trot.

Even as the crow flies, or the bee wings its flight, the length of Benee's journey would be over six hundred miles. But it was impossible for anyone to keep a bee-line, owing to the roughness of the country and the difficulties of every kind to be overcome, so that it is indeed impossible to estimate the magnitude of this lone Indian's exploit.

His way, roughly speaking, lay between the Madeira River and the Great Snake River called Puras (*vide* map); latterly it would lead him to the lofty regions and plateaux of the head-waters of Maya-tata, called by the Peruvians the Madre de Dios, or Holy Virgin River.

But hardly a day now passed that he had not a stream of some kind to cross, and wandering by its banks seeking for a ford delayed him considerably.

He was journeying thus one morning when the sound of human voices not far off made him creep quickly into the jungle.

The men did not take long to put in an appearance.

A portion of some wandering, hunting, or looting tribe they were, and cut-throat looking scoundrels everyone of them—five in all.

They were armed with bows and arrows and with spears. Their arrows, Benee could see, were tipped with flint, and the flint was doubtless poisoned. They carried also slings and broad knives in their belts of skin. The slings are used in warfare, but they are also used by shepherds—monsters who, like many in this country, know not the meaning of the words "mercy to dumb animals"—on their poor sheep.

These fellows, who now lay down to rest and to eat, much to Benee's disgust, not to say dismay, were probably a party of llama (pronounced yahmah) herds or shepherds who had, after cutting their master's throat, banded together and taken to this roving life.

So thought Benee, at all events, for he could see many articles of European dress, such as dainty scarves of silk, lace handkerchiefs, &c., as well as brooches, huddled over their own clothing, and one fierce-looking fellow pulled out a gold watch and pretended to look at the time.

So angry was Benee that his savage nature got uppermost, and he handled his huge revolvers in a nervous way that showed his anxiety to open fire and spoil the cut-throats' dinner. But he restrained himself for the time being.

In addition to the two revolvers, Benee carried the repeating rifle. It was the fear of spoiling his ammunition that led to his being in this dreadful fix. But for his cartridges he could have swum the river with the speed of a garfish.

What a long, long time they stayed, and how very leisurely they munched and fed!

A slight sound on his left flank caused Benee to gaze hastily round. To his horror, he found himself face to face with a puma.

Here was indeed a dilemma!

If he fired he would make his presence known, and small mercy could he expect from the cut-throats. At all hazards he determined to keep still.

The yellow eyes of this American lion flared and glanced in a streak of sunshine shot downwards through the bush, and it was this probably which dimmed his vision, for he made no attempt to spring forward.

Benee dared scarcely to breathe; he could hear the beating of his own heart, and could not help wondering if the puma heard it too.

At last the brute backed slowly astern, with a wriggling motion.

But Benee gained courage now.

During the long hours that followed, several great snakes passed him so closely that he could have touched their scaly backs. Some of these were lithe and long, others very thick and slow in motion, but nearly all were beautifully coloured in metallic tints of crimson, orange, green, and bronze, and all were poisonous.

The true Bolivian, however, has but little fear of snakes, knowing that unless trodden upon, or otherwise actively interfered with, they care not to waste their venom by striking.

At long, long last the cut-throats got up to leave. They would before midnight no doubt reach some lonely outpost and demand entertainment at the point of the knife, and if strange travellers were there, sad indeed would be their fate.

Benee now crawled, stiff and cramped, out from his damp and dangerous hiding-place. He found a ford not far off, and after crossing, he set off once more at his swinging trot, and was soon supple and happy enough.

On and on he went all that day, to make up for lost time, and far into the starry night.

The hills were getting higher now, the valleys deeper and damper between, and stream after stream had to be forded.

It must have been long past eight o'clock when, just as Benee was beginning to long for food and rest, his eyes fell on a glimmering light at the foot of a high and dark precipice.

He warily ventured forward and found it proceeded from a shepherd's hut; inside sat the man himself, quietly eating a kind of thick soup, the basin flanked by a huge flagon of milk, with roasted yams. Great, indeed, was the innocent fellow's surprise when Benee presented himself in the doorway. A few words in Bolivian, kindly uttered by our wayfarer, immediately put the man at ease, however, and before long Benee was enjoying a hearty supper, followed by a brew of excellent maté.

He was a very simple son of the desert, this shepherd, but a desultory kind of conversation was maintained, nevertheless, until far into the night.

For months and months, he told Benee, he had lived all alone with his sheep in these grassy uplands, having only the companionship of his half-wild, but faithful dog. But he was contented and happy, and had plenty to eat and drink.

It was just sunrise when Benee awoke from a long refreshing sleep on his bed of skins. There was the odour of smoke all about, and presently the shepherd himself bustled in and bade him "Good-morning!", or "Heaven's blessing!" which is much the same.

A breakfast of rough, black cake, with butter, fried fish, and maté, made Benee as happy as a king and as fresh as a mountain trout, and soon after he said farewell and started once more on his weary road. The only regret he experienced rose from the fact that he had nothing wherewith to reward this kindly shepherd for his hospitality.

Much against his will, our wanderer had now to make a long detour, for not even a goat could have scaled the ramparts of rock in front of him.

In another week he found himself in one of the bleakest and barrenest stretches of country that it is possible to imagine. It was a high plateau, and covered for the most part with stunted bushes and with crimson heath and heather.

Benee climbed a high hill that rose near him, and as he stood on the top thereof, just as the sun in a glory of orange clouds and crimson rose slowly and majestically over the far-off eastern forest, a scene presented itself to him that, savage though he was, caused him for a time to stand mute with admiration and wonder.

Then he remembered what little Peggy told him once in her sweet and serious voice: "Always pray at sunrise".

> "Always pray at sunrise,
>
> For 'tis God who makes the day;
>
> When shades of evening gather round
>
> Kneel down again and pray.
>
> And He, who loves His children dear,
>
> Will send some angel bright
>
> To guard you while you're sleeping sound
>
> And watch you all the night."

And on this lonely hill-top Benee did kneel down to pray a simple prayer, while golden clouds were changing to bronze and snowy white, and far off on the forest lands hazy vapours were still stretched across glens and valleys.

As he rose from his knees he could hear, away down beneath him, a wild shout, and gazing in the direction from which it came, he saw seven semi-nude savages hurrying towards the mountain with the evident intention of making him prisoner.

It was terrible odds; but as there was no escape, Benee determined to fight.

As usual, they were armed with bow and arrow and sling.

Indeed, they commenced throwing stones with great precision before they reached the hill-foot, and one of these fell at Benee's feet.

Glad, indeed, was he next minute to find himself in a kind of natural trench which could have been held by twenty men against a hundred.

On and up, crawling on hands and knees, came the savages.

But Benee stood firm, rifle in hand, and waiting his chance.

# CHAPTER XII—BENEE ENTRENCHED— SAVAGE REVELS IN THE FOREST

The trench in which he found himself was far higher than was necessary, and fronted by huge stones. It was evidently the work of human hands, but by what class of people erected Benee could not imagine.

He could spare a few boulders anyhow, so, while the enemy was still far below, he started first one, then another, and still another, on a cruise down the mountain-side and on a mission of death.

These boulders broke into scores of large fragments long before they reached the savages, two of whom were struck, one being killed outright.

And Benee knew his advantage right well, and, taking careful aim now with his repeating-rifle—a sixteen-shooter it was,—he fired.

He saw the bullet raise the dust some yards ahead of the foe, who paused to gaze upwards in great amazement.

But next shot went home, for Benee had got the range, and one of the five threw up his hands with a shriek, and fell on his face, to rise no more.

Rendered wild by the loss of their companions, the others drew their knives and made a brave start for Benee's trench.

But what could poor savages do against the deadly fire of civilized warfare. When another of their number paid the penalty of his rashness, the other three took fright and went racing and tumbling down the hill so quickly that no more of Benee's shots took effect.

Roland had given Benee a field-glass before he started, and through this he watched the flying figures for many a mile, noting exactly the way they took, and determining in his own mind to choose a somewhat different route, even though he should have to make a wide detour.

He started downhill almost immediately, well-knowing that these dark-skinned devils would return reinforced to seek revenge.

He knew, moreover, that they could follow up a trail, so he did all in his power to pick out the hardest parts of this great moorland on which to walk.

He came at last to a stream. It was very shallow, and he plunged in at once.

This was indeed good luck, and Benee thought now that Peggy's God, who paints the sky at sunrise, was really looking after him. He could baulk his pursuers now, or, at least, delay them. For they would not be able to tell in which direction he had gone.

So Benee walked in the water for three miles. This walk was really a leaping run. He would have gone farther, but all at once the stream became very rapid indeed, and on his ears fell the boom of a waterfall.

So he got on shore with all haste.

But for five miles on from the foot of the leaping, dashing, foaming linn, the stream was flanked by acres of round, smooth boulders.

These could tell no tale. On these Benee would leave no trail. He leapt from one to the other, and was rejoiced at last to find that they led him to a forest.

This was indeed a grateful surprise, so he entered the shade at once.

Benee, after his exciting fight and his very long run, greatly needed rest, so he gathered some splendid fruit and nuts, despite the chattering and threatened attacks of a whole band of hideous baboons, and then threw himself down under the shade of a tree in a small glade and made a hearty meal.

He felt thirsty now. But as soon as there was silence once more in the forest, and even the parrots had gone to sleep in the drowsy noontide heat, he could hear the rush of water some distance ahead.

He got up immediately and marched in the direction from which the sound came, and was soon on the pebbled shore of another burn.

He drank a long, sweet draught of the cool, delicious water, and felt wondrously refreshed.

And now a happy thought occurred to him.

Sooner or later he felt certain the savages would find his trail. They would track him to this stream and believe he had once again tried to break the pursuit by wading either up or down stream.

His plan was, therefore, to go carefully back on his tracks and rest hidden all day until, foiled in their attempt to make him prisoner, they should return homeward.

This plan he carried into immediate execution, and in a thicket, quite screened from all observation, he laid him down.

He was soon fast asleep.

But in probably a couple of hours' time he sat cautiously up, and, gently lifting a branch, looked forth.

For voices had fallen on his ear, and next minute there went filing past on his trail no fewer than fifteen well-armed warriors.

They stopped dancing and shouting at the tree where Benee had sat down to feed, then, brandishing their broad knives, dashed forward to the stream.

They had evidently gone up the river for miles, but finding no trail on the other bank returned to search the down-stream.

In his hiding-place Benee could hear their wild shouts of vengeance-deferred, and though he feared not death, right well he knew that neither his rifle nor revolvers could long protect him against such desperate odds as this.

There was now peace once more, and the shades of evening—the short tropical gloaming—were falling when he heard the savages returning.

He knew their language well.

It was soon evident that they did not mean to go any farther that night, for they were quite tired out.

They were not unprovided with food and drink such as it was, and evidently meant to make themselves happy.

A fire was soon lit in the glade, and by its glare poor Benee, lying low there and hardly daring to move a limb, could see the sort of savages he would have to deal with if they found him.

They were fierce-looking beyond conception. Most of them had long matted hair, and the ears of some carried the hideous pelele. The lobe of each ear is pierced when the individual is but a boy, and is gradually stretched until it is a mere strip of skin capable of supporting a bone or wooden, grooved little wheel twice as large as a dollar. The stretched lobe of the ear fits round this like the tyre round a bicycle wheel.

The faces of these men, although wild-looking, were not positively ill-favoured, though the mouths were large and sensual. But if ever devil lurked in human eyes it lurked in theirs.

They wore blankets, and some had huge chains of gold and silver nuggets round their necks.

Their arms were now piled, or, more correctly speaking, they were trundled down in a heap by the tree.

While most of them lay with their feet to the now roaring fire, a space was left for the cook, who cleverly arranged a kind of gipsy double-trident over the clear embers and commenced to get ready the meal.

The uprights carried cross pieces of wood, and on these both fish and flesh were laid to broil, while large yams and sweet-potatoes were placed in the ashes to roast.

By the time dinner was cooked the night was dark enough, but the glimmer of the firelight lit up the savages' faces and cast Rembrandtesque shadows far behind.

It was a weird and terrible scene, but it had little effect on Benee, who had often witnessed tableaux far more terrifying than this.

Then the orgie commenced. They helped themselves with their fingers and tore the fish and flesh off with their splendid teeth.

Huge chattees of chicaga, a most filthy but intoxicating beer, now made their appearance. It was evident enough that these men were used to being on the war-path and hunting-field.

The wine or beer is made in a very disgusting manner, but its manufacture, strangely enough, is not confined to Bolivia. I have seen much the same liquor in tropical Africa, made by the Somali Indians, and in precisely the same way.

The old women or hags of the village are assembled at, say, a chief's house, and large quantities of cocoanuts and various other fruits are heaped together in the centre of a hut, as well as large, tub-like vessels and chattees of water.

Down the old and almost toothless hags squat, and, helping themselves to lumps of cocoa-nut, &c., they commence to mumble and chew these, now and then moistening their mouths with a little water, the juice is spit out into calabashes, and when these are full of the awful mess they are emptied into the big bin.

It is a great gala-day with these hideous old hags, a meeting that they take advantage of not only for making wine but for abusing their neighbours.

How they cackle and grin, to be sure, as their mouths work to and fro! How they talk and chatter, and how they chew! It is chatter and chew, chew and chatter, all the time, and the din they make with teeth and tongues would deafen a miller.

When all is finished, the bins are left to settle and ferment, and in three days' time, the supernatant liquor is poured off and forms the wine called chicaga.

Had anyone doubted the intoxicating power of this vilest of all vile drinks, a glance at the scene which soon ensued around the fire would speedily have convinced him.

Benee lay there watching these fiends as they gradually merged from one phase of drunkenness to another, and fain would he have sent half a dozen revolver bullets into the centre of the group, but his life depended on his keeping still.

The savages first confined themselves to merry talking, with coarse jokes and ribaldry, and frequent outbursts of laughter. But when they had quaffed still more, they must seize their knives and get up to dance. Round and round the blazing fire they whirled and staggered through the smoke and through it again, with demoniacal shouts and awful yells, that awakened echoes among the forest wild beasts far and near.

Then they pricked their bodies with their knives till the blood ran, and with this they splashed each other in hideous wantonness till faces and clothes were smeared in gore.

All this could but have one ending—a fight.

Benee saw one savage stabbed to the heart, and then the orgie became a fierce battle.

Now was Benee's time to escape.

Yet well he knew how acute the power of hearing is among the Bolivian savages. One strange noise, even the crackle of a bush, and the fighting would end in a hunt, and he would undoubtedly lose his life.

But he wriggled and crawled like a snake in the grass until twenty yards away, and now he moved cautiously, slowly off.

Soon the glare of the fire among the high trees was seen no more, and the yelling and cries were far behind and getting more and more indistinct every minute.

Benee refreshed himself at the stream, pulled some food from his pocket, and ate it while he ran.

He knew, however, that after fighting would come drowsiness, and that his late entertainers would soon be fast asleep, some of their heads pillowed, perhaps, on the dead body of their murdered comrade.

If there be in all this world a more demonish wretch than man is in a state of nature, or when—even among Christians—demoralized by drink, I wish to get hold of a specimen for my private menagerie. But the creature should be kept in a cage by itself. I would not insult my monkeys with the companionship of such a wretch, should it be man or beast.

# CHAPTER XIII—THE MARCH TO THE LOVELESS LAND

On and on hurried Benee now, at his old swinging trot.

On and on beneath the splendid stars, his only companions, that looked so calmly sweet and appeared so near. God's angels surely they, speaking, as they gazed down, words from their home on high, peace and good-will to men, and happiness to all that lived and breathed.

On and on over plains, through moor and marsh, by lake and stream, by forest dark and jungle wild. It was evident that Benee meant to put leagues between himself and the camp of his recent enemies before each star grew beautiful and died; before the fiery sun leapt red above the eastern hills, and turned the darkness into day.

Benee had come onwards with such a rush that even the slimy alligators, by pond or brown lake, left their lairs among the tall nodding reeds and dashed in terror into the water.

Prowling wild beasts, the jaguar and puma, also hurried off at his approach, and many a scared bird flew screaming up into the darkling air.

But Benee heeded nothing. His way lay yonder. That bright particular star away down on the southwestern horizon shone over the great unexplored region of Bolivia.

Morning after morning it would be higher and higher above him, and when it shone at an angle of forty-five degrees he would be approaching the land of the cannibals.

Yes, but it was still a far cry to that country. By the time the sun did rise, and the mists gathered themselves off the valleys and glens that lay low beneath him, Benee felt sadly in want of rest.

He found a tree that would make him a good sleeping place, for the country he was now traversing abounded in hideous snakes and gigantic lizards, and he courted not the companionship of either.

The tree was an Abies of some undefined species.

Up and up crawled Benee, somewhat encumbered by his arms.

He got through a kind of "lubbers' hole" at last, though with much difficulty, and, safe enough here, he curled up with his face to the stem, and was soon so fast asleep that cannons could not have awakened him.

But satisfied Nature got uneasy at last, and far on towards evening he opened his eyes and wondered where he was.

Still only half-awake, he staggered to his feet and made a step forward. It was only to fall over the end of a huge matted branch, but this branch lowered him gently on to the one immediately beneath it, and this down to the next, and so on. A strange mode of progression certainly, but Benee found himself sitting on the ground at last, as safe and sound as if he had come down in a parachute.

Then his recollection came back to him. He sought out some fruit-trees now and made a hearty meal, quenched his thirst at a spring, and once more resumed his journey.

For three days he marched onwards, but always by night. The country was not safe by day, and he preferred the companionship of wild beasts to that of wilder men. In this Benee was wise.

But awaking somewhat earlier one afternoon, he saw far beneath him, a town, and in Benee's eyes it was a very large one.

And now a happy idea struck him. He had money, and here was civilization. By and by he would be in the wilds once more, and among savages who knew nothing of cash. Why should he not descend, mix with the giddy throng, and make purchases of red cloth, of curios, and of beads. He determined to do so.

But it would not do to go armed. So he hid his rifle and pistols in the bush, covering them carefully up with dried grass. Then he commenced the descent. Yes, the little town, the greater part of which was built of mud hovels, was full, and the streets crowded, many in the throng being Spaniards, Peruvians, and Portuguese.

Benee sauntered carelessly on and presently came to the bazaar.

Many of the police eyed him curiously, and one or two followed him.

But he had no intention of being baulked in his purpose.

So he entered a likely shop, and quickly made his purchases.

Wrapping these carefully up, he slung the bundle over his shoulder and left.

He stumbled over a lanky Portuguese policeman a few yards off.

The man would have fallen had not Benee seized him in his iron grasp and brought him again to his equilibrium.

Then he spoke a few words in Bolivian, and made signs that he wished to eat and drink.

"Aguardiente!" said the officer, his eyes sparkling with joy.

He had really harboured some intentions of throwing Benee into the tumble-down old prison, but a drink would be a far better solution of the difficulty, and he cheerfully led the way to a sort of hotel.

And in twenty minutes' time this truly intelligent member of the force and Benee were lying on skin mats with apparently all the good things in this life spread out before them.

The officer was curious, as all such men are, whether heathens or not, to know all about Benee, and put to him a score of questions at least, part of which Benee replied to with a delicate and forgivable fib.

So the policeman was but little wiser at the end of the conversation than he was at the beginning.

About half an hour before sunset, Benee was once more far up on the moorlands, and making straight for the place where he had hidden his guns and ammunition.

But he stopped short and stared with astonishment when, before rounding the corner of the wood, a pistol shot rang out in the quiet air, followed by the most terrible shrieking and howling he had ever listened to.

He hurried on quickly enough now, and as he did so, a whole herd of huge monkeys, apparently scared out of their senses, rushed madly past him.

Close to the jungle he found one of his revolvers. One chamber had been emptied, and not far off lay a baboon in the agonies of death. Benee, who, savage though he was, evidently felt for the creature, mercifully expended another shot on it, and placed it beyond the reach of woe.

He was glad to find his rifle and other revolver intact, but the cartridges from his belt were scattered about in all directions, and strenuous efforts had evidently been made to tear open his leathern ammunition-box.

It took some time to make everything straight again.

Now down went the sun, and very soon, after a short twilight, out came the stars once more.

Benee now resumed his journey as straight as he could across the plateau.

He had not travelled many hours, however, before clouds began to bank up and obscure the sky, and it became very dark.

A storm was brewing, and, ushered in by low muttering thunder in the far distance, it soon came on in earnest.

As the big drops of rain began to fall, shining in the flashes of the lightning like a shower of molten gold, Benee sought the shelter of a rocky cave which was near to him.

He laid him down on the rough dry grass to wait until the storm should clear away.

He felt drowsy, however. Perhaps the unusually good fare he had partaken of in the village had something to do with this; but of late his hardships had been very great indeed, so it is no wonder that now exhausted Nature claimed repose.

The last thing he was conscious of was a long, low, mournful cry that seemed to come from the far interior of the cave.

It was broad daylight when he again awoke, and such an awakening!

Great snowy-breasted owls sat blinking at the light, but all the rocks around, or the shelves thereof, were alive with coiling, wriggling snakes of huge size.

One had twined round his leg, and he knew that if he but moved a muscle, it would send its terrible fangs deep into his flesh, and his journey would be at an end.

Gradually, however, the awful creature unwound itself and wriggled away.

The sight of this snake-haunted cave was too much for even Benee's nerves, and he sprang up and speedily dashed, all intact, into the open air.

———

Notwithstanding his extraordinary adventure in the cave of serpents, the wandering Indian felt in fine form that day.

The air was now much cooler after the storm, all the more so, no doubt, that Benee was now travelling on a high table-land which stretched southwards and west in one long, dreary expanse till bounded on the horizon by ridges of lofty serrated mountains, in the hollow of which, high in air, patches of snow rested, and probably had so rested for millions of years.

The sky was very bright. The trees at this elevation, as well as the fruit, the flowers, and stunted shrubs, were just such as one finds at the Cape of

Good Hope and other semi-tropical regions. The ground on which he walked or trotted along was a mass of beauty and perfume, rich pink or crimson heaths, heather and geraniums everywhere, with patches of pine-wood having little or no undergrowth. Many rare and beautiful birds lilted and sang their songs of love on every side, strange larks were high in air, some lighting every now and then on the ground, the music of their voices drawn out as they glided downwards into one long and beautiful cadence.

There seemed to be a sadness in these last notes, as if the birds would fain have warbled for ever and for aye at heaven's high gate, though duty drew them back to this dull earth of ours.

But dangers to these feathered wildlings hovered even in the sunlit sky, and sometimes turned the songs of those speckled-breasted laverocks into wails of despair.

Behold yonder hawk silently darting from the pine-wood! High, high he darts into the air; he has positioned his quarry, and downwards now he swoops like Indian arrow from a bow, and the lark's bright and happy song is hushed for ever. His beautiful mate sitting on her cosy nest with its five brown eggs looks up astonished and frightened. Down fall a few drops of red blood, as if the sky had wept them. Down flutter a few feathers, and her dream of happiness is a thing of the past.

And that poor widowed lark will forsake her eggs now, and wander through the heath and the scrub till she dies.

––––––––

Benee had no adventures to-day, but, seeing far off a band of travellers, he hid himself in the afternoon. For our Indian wanted no company.

He watched them as they came rapidly on towards his hiding-place, but they struck off to the east long before reaching it, and made for the plains and village far below.

Then Benee had his dinner and slept soundly enough till moonrise, for bracing and clear was heaven's ozonic breath in these almost Alpine regions.

Only a scimitar of a moon. Not more than three days old was it, yet somehow it gave hope and heart to the lonely traveller. He remembered when a boy he had been taught to look upon the moon as a good angel, but Christianity had banished superstition, and he was indeed a new man.

After once more refreshing himself, he started on his night march, hoping to put forty miles behind him ere the sun rose.

Low lay the white haze over the woods a sheer seven thousand feet beneath him.

It looked like snow-drifts on the darkling green.

Yet here and there, near to places where the river glistened in the young moon's rays were bunches of lights, and Benee knew he was not far from towns and civilization. Much too near to be agreeable.

He knew, however, that a few days more of his long weary march would bring him far away from these to regions unknown to the pale-face, to a land on which Christian feet had never trodden, a loveless land, a country that reeked with murder, a country that seemed unblessed by heaven, where all was moral darkness, as if indeed it were ruled by demons and fiends, who rejoiced only in the spilling of blood.

But, nevertheless, it was Benee's own land, and he could smile while he gazed upwards at the now descending moon.

Benee never felt stronger or happier than he did this evening, and he sang a strange wild song to himself, as he journeyed onwards, a kind of chant to which he kept step.

A huge snake, black as a winter's night, uncoiled itself, hissed, and darted into the heath to hide. Benee heeded it not. A wild beast of some sort sprang past him with furious growl. Benee never even raised his rifle. And when he came to the banks of a reed-girt lake, and saw his chance of shooting a huge cayman, he cared not to draw a bead thereon. He just went on with his chant and on with his walk. Benee was truly happy and hopeful for once in his life.

And amid such scenery, beneath such a galaxy of resplendent stars, who could have been aught else?

> "How beautiful is night!
>
> A dewy freshness fills the silent air;
>
> No mist obscures, nor cloud, nor speck, nor stain,
>
> Breaks the serene of heaven.
>
> In glory yonder moon divine
>
> Rolls through the dark-blue depths,
>
> Beneath her steely ray
>
> The desert circle spreads,
>
> Like the round ocean girdled with the sky.
>
> How beautiful the night!"

But almost before he could have believed it possible, so quickly do health and happiness cause time to fly, a long line of crimson cloud, high in the east, betokened the return of another day.

The night-owls and the great flitting vampire bats saw it and retreated to darksome caves. There was heard no longer far over the plain the melancholy howl of the tiger-cat or snarl of puma or jaguar.

Day was coming!

Day was come!

# CHAPTER XIV—THE HOME OF THE CANNIBAL—BENEE'S ROMANCE

Like the bats and the night-birds Benee now crept into concealment.

He sought once more the shelter of a tall pine-tree of the spruce species. Here he could be safe and here he could sleep.

But after a hearty meal he took the precaution to lash himself to the stem, high, high up.

His descent from the last tree had been accomplished with safety certainly, but it was of rather a peculiar nature, and Benee had no desire to risk his neck again.

The wind softly sighed in the branches.

A bird of the thrush species alighted about a yard above him, and burst into shrill sweet melody to welcome the rising sun.

With half-closed eyes Benee could see from under the branches a deep-orange horizon, fading into pure sea-green zenithwards, then to deepest purple and blue where rested the crimson clouds.

And now there was a glare of brighter and more silvery light, and the red streaks were turned into wreaths of snow.

The sun was up, and Benee slept. But he carried that sweet bird's song into dreamland.

---

About three days after this Benee was rejoiced to find himself in a new land, but it was a land he knew well—too well.

Though very high above the sea-level it was in reality a

"Land of the mountain and the flood".


Hills on hills rose on all sides of him. There were straths or valleys of such exceeding beauty that they gladdened the eye to behold. The grass grew green here by the banks of many a brown roaring stream, and here, too, cattle roamed wild and free, knee-deep in flowery verdure, and many a beautiful guanaco and herds of llamas everywhere. The streams that meandered through these highland straths were sometimes very tortuous, but perhaps a mile distant they would seem to lose all control of themselves and go madly rushing over their pebbly beds, till they dashed over high cliffs at last, forming splendid cascades that fell into deep, dark, agitated pools, the mist that rose above forming rainbows which were never absent when the sun shone.

And the hillsides that bounded these valleys were clad in Alpine verdure, with Alpine trees and flowers, strangely intermingled with beautiful heaths, and in the open glades with gorgeous geraniums, and many a lovely flower never seen even in greenhouses in our "tame domestic England".

These were valleys, but there were glens and narrow gorges also, where dark beetling rocks frowned over the brown waters of streams that rushed fiercely onwards round rocks and boulders, against which they lashed themselves into foam.

On these rocks strange fantastic trees clung, sometimes attached but by the rootlets, sometimes with their heads hanging almost sheer downwards; trees that the next storm of wind would hurl, with crash and roar, into the water far beneath.

Yet such rivers or big burns were the home *par excellence* of fish of the salmon tribe, and gazing below you might see here and there some huge otter, warily watching to spring on his finny prey.

Nor were the otters alone on the *qui vive*, for, strange as it may seem, even pumas and tiger-cats often made a sullen dive into dark-brown pools, and emerged bearing on high some lordly red-bellied fish. With this they would "speel" the flowery, ferny rocks, and dart silently away into the depths of the forest.

And this wild and beautiful country, at present inhabited by as wild a race of Indians as ever twanged the bow, but bound at no very distant date to come under the influence of Christianity and civilization, was Benee's real home. 'Twas here he roamed when a boy, for he had been a wanderer all his life, a nomad, and an inhabitant of the woods and wilds.

Not a scene was unfamiliar to him. He could name every mountain and hill he gazed upon in his own strangely musical Indian tongue. Every bird, every creature that crept, or glided, or walked, all were his old friends; yes, and every tree and every flower, from the splendid parasitic plants that wound around the trees wherever the sun shone the brightest, and draped them in such a wealth of beauty as would have made all the richness and gaudiness of white kings and queens seem but a caricature.

There was something of romance even in Benee. As he stood with folded arms on the brink of a cliff, and gazed downward into a charming glen, something very like tears stood in his eyes.

He loved his country. It was his own, his native land. But the savages therein he had ceased to love. Because when but a boy—ah, how well he remembered that day,—he was sent one day by his father and mother to gather the berries of a deadly kind of thorn-bush, with the juice of which the flints in the points of the arrows were poisoned. Coming back to his parents' hut in the evening, as happy as boys only can be, he found the place in flames, and saw his father, mother, and a sister whom he loved, being hurried away by the savages, because the queen had need of them. The lot of death had fallen on them. Their flesh was wanted to make part of a great feast her majesty was about to give to a neighbouring potentate. Benee, who had ever been used to hunt for his food as a boy, or fish in the lakes and the brown roaring streams, that he and his parents might live, had always abhorred human sacrifice and human flesh. The latter he had seldom been prevailed upon even to taste.

So from that terrible day he resolved to be a wanderer, and he registered a vow—if I may speak so concerning the thoughts of a poor boy-Indian—to take revenge when he became a man on this very tribe that had brought such grief and woe on him and his.

Benee was still a young man, but little over two-and-twenty, and as he stood there thoughts came into his mind about a little sweetheart he had when a boy.

Wee Weenah was she called; only a child of six when he was good sixteen. But in all his adventures, in forest or by the streams, Weenah used to accompany him. They used to be away together all day long, and lived on the nuts and the wild fruit that grew everywhere so plentifully about them, on trees, on bushes, or on the flowery banks.

Where was Weenah now? Dead, perhaps, or taken away to the queen's blood-stained court. As a child Weenah was very beautiful, for many of these Indians are very far indeed from being repulsive.

And Benee used to delight to dress his tiny lady-love in feathers of the wild birds, crimson and green and blue, and weave her rude garlands of the gaudiest flowers, to hang around her neck, or entwine in her long dark hair.

He had gone to see Weenah—though he was then in grief and tears—after he had left his father's burnt shealing. He had told her that he was going away far to the north, that he was to become a hunter of the wilds, that he might even visit the homes of the white men, but that some day he would return and Weenah should be his wife.

So they had parted thus, in childish grief and tears, and he had never seen her since.

He might see her nevermore.

While musing thus to himself, he stretched his weary limbs and body on

116

the sweet-scented mossy cliff-top.

It was day certainly, but was he not now at home, in his own, his native land?

He seemed to be afraid of nothing, therefore, and so—he fell asleep.

The bank on which he slept adjoined a darkling forest.

A forest of strange dark pines, with red-brown stems, which, owing to the absence of all undergrowth save heather and moss and fern, looked like the pillars of some vast cavern.

But there was bird music in this forest, and Benee had gone to sleep with the flute-like and mellow notes of the soo-soo falling on his ear.

The soo-soo's song had accompanied him to the land of forgetfulness, and was mingling even now with his dreams—happy dreams of long ago.

But list! Was that really the song of the bronze-necked soo-soo?

He was half-awake now, but apparently dreaming still.

He thought he was dreaming at all events, and would not have opened his eyes and so dispelled the dream for all the world.

It was a sweet girlish voice that seemed to be singing—singing about him, about Benee the wanderer in sylvan wilds; the man who for long years had been alone because he loved being alone, whose hand—until he reached the white man's home—had been against everyone, and against every beast as well.

And the song was a kind of sweet little ballad, which I should try in vain to translate.

But Benee opened his eyes at last, and his astonishment knew no bounds as he saw, kneeling by his mossy couch, the self-same Weenah that he had been thinking and dreaming about.

Though still a girl in years, being but thirteen, she seemed a woman in all her sympathies.

Beautiful? Yes; scarcely changed as to face from the child of six he used to roam in the woods with in the long, long ago. Her dark hair hung to her waist and farther in two broad plaits. Her black eyes brimmed over with joy, and there was a flush of excitement on her sun-kissed cheeks.

"Weenah! Oh, Weenah! Can it be you?" he exclaimed in the Indian tongue.

"It is your own little child-love, your Weenah; and ah! how I have longed for you, and searched for you far and near. See, I am clad in the skins of the puma and the otter; I have killed the jaguar, too, and I have been far north and fought with terrible men. They fell before the poison of my arrows. They tried to catch me; but fleet of foot is Weenah, and they never can see me when I fly. In trees I have slept, on the open heather, in caves of rocks, and in jungle. But never, never could I find my Benee. Ah! life of mine, you will never go and leave us again.

"Yes," she added, "Mother and Father live, and are well. Our home have we enlarged. 'Tis big now, and there is room in it for Benee.

"Come; come—shall we go? But what strange, strange war-weapons you carry. Ah! they are the fire-spears of the white man."

"Yes, Weenah mine! and deadly are they as the lightning's bolt that flashes downward from the storm-sky and lays dead the llama and the ox.

"See yonder eagle, Weenah? Benee's aim is unerring; his hand is the hand of the rock, his eye the eye of the kron-dah" (a kind of hawk), "yet his touch on the trigger light as the moss-flax. Behold!"

He raised the rifle as he spoke, and without even appearing to take aim he fired.

Next moment the bird of Jove turned a somersault. It was a death-spasm. Down, down he fell earthwards, his breast-feathers following more slowly, like a shower of snow sparkling in the sunshine.

Weenah was almost paralysed with terror, but Benee took her gently in his arms, and, kissing her brow and bonnie raven hair, soothed her and stilled her alarms.

Hand in hand now through the forest, as in the days of yore! Both almost too happy to speak, Benee and his little Indian maiden! Hand in hand over the plain, through the crimson heath and the heather, heeding nothing, seeing nothing, knowing nothing save their own great happiness! Hand in hand until they stood beside Weenah's mother's cottage; and her parents soon ran out to welcome and to bless them!

Theirs was no ordinary hut, for the father had been far to the east and had dwelt among white men on the banks of the rapid-rolling Madeira.

When he had returned, slaves had come with him—young men whom he had bought, for the aborigines barter their children for cloth or schnapps. And these slaves brought with them tools of the white men—axes, saws, adzes, hammers, spades, and shovels.

Then Shooks-gee (swift of foot) had cut himself timber from the forest, and, aided by his slaves, had set to work; and lo! in three moons this cottage by the wood arose, and the queen of the cannibals herself had none better.

But Benee was welcomed and food set before him, milk of the llama, corn-cakes, and eggs of the heron and treel-ba (a kind of plover).

Then warm drinks of coca (not cocoa) were given him, and the child Weenah's eyes were never turned away while he ate and drank.

He smoked then, the girl sitting close by him on the bench and watching the strange, curling rings of reek rolling upwards towards the black and glittering rafters.

"But," said Weenah's mother, "poor Benee has walked far and is much tired. Would not Benee like to cover his feet?"

"Yes, our mother, Benee would sleep."

"And I will watch and sing," said Weenah.

"Sing the song of the forest," murmured Benee.

Then Weenah sang low beside him while Benee slept.

# CHAPTER XV—SHOOKS-GEE'S STORY—A CANNIBAL QUEEN

What is called "natural curiosity" in our country, where almost every man is a Paul Pry, is no trait of the Indian's character. Or if he ever does feel such an impulse, it is instantly checked. Curiosity is but the attribute of a squaw, a savage would tell you, but even squaws will try to prevent such a weed from flourishing in their hearts.

That was the reason why neither the father nor the mother of Benee's little lady-love thought of asking him a single question concerning his adventures until he had eaten a hearty meal and had enjoyed a refreshing sleep.

But when Benee sat up at last and quaffed the maté that Weenah had made haste to get him, and just as the day was beginning to merge into the twilight of summer, he began to tell his friends and his love some portion of his wonderful adventures, even from the day when he had bidden the child Weenah a tearful farewell and betaken himself to a wandering life in the woods.

His young life's story was indeed a strange one,

> "Wherein he spake of most disastrous chances,
>
> Of moving accidents by flood and field;
>
> … of antres vast and deserts idle,
>
> Rough quarries, rocks, and hills whose heads touch heaven.

---

The while Weenah

"… gave him for his pains a world of sighs.

'T was strange, 't was passing strange,

'T was pitiful, 't was wondrous pitiful:

She wished she had not heard it; yet she wished

That heaven had made her such a man."

Then when Benee came down to that portion of his long story when first he found the children and their mighty wolf-hound lost in the forest, Weenah and her parents listened with greater interest and intensity than ever.

There was a fire on the rude, low hearth—a fire of wood, of peat, and of moss; for at the great elevation at which this cannibal land is situated the nights are chilly.

It was a fire that gave fitful light as well as heat. It fell on the faces of Benee's listeners, and cast shadows grotesque behind them. It beautified Weenah's face till Benee thought she looked like one of the angels that poor Peggy used to tell him about.

Then he related to them all his suspicions of Peter, but did not actually accuse him of bringing about the abduction of Peggy, to serve some vile and unknown purpose of his own. Next he spoke, yet spoke but lightly, of his long, long march, and the incidents and adventures therewith connected.

There was much, therefore, that Benee had to tell, but there was also much that he had to learn or to be told; and now that he had finished, it was Shooks-gee's turn to take up the story.

I wish I could do justice to this man's language, which was grandly figurative, or to his dramatic way of talking, accompanied as it was with look and gesture that would have elicited applause on any European stage. I cannot do so, therefore shall not try; but the following is the pith of his story.

This Indian's house was on the very outside and most northerly end of the great wild plateau which was the home of these savages and cannibals.

The queen, a terrible monarch, and bloodthirsty in the extreme, used to hold her court and lived on a strange mountain or hill, in the very centre of the rough tree and bush clad plain.

For many, many a long year she had lived here, and to her court Indians came from afar to do her homage, bringing with them cloth of crimson, wine and oil, which they had stolen or captured in warfare from the white men of Madeira valley.

When these presents came, the coca which her courtiers used to chew all day long, and the maté they drank, were for a time—for weeks indeed—discarded for the wine and fire-water of the pale-face.

Fearful were the revels then held on that lone mountain.

The queen was dainty, so too were her fierce courtiers.

When the revels first began she and they could eat the raw or half-roasted flesh of calves and baby-llamas, but when their potations waxed deeper, and appetite began to fail, then the orgies commenced in earnest. Nothing would her majesty eat now—horrible to say—but children, and her courtiers, armed to the teeth, would be sent to scour the plains, to visit the mud huts of her people, and drag therefrom the most beautiful and plump boys or girls procurable.

I will not tell of the fearful and awfully unnatural human sacrifice—the murder of the innocents—that now took place.

Demons could not have been more revolting in their cruelties than were those savage courtiers as they obeyed the queen's behests.

Let me drop the curtain over this portion of the tale. Well, this particular cottage or hut, being on the confines of the country, had not been visited by the queen's fearsome soldiers. But even had they come they would have found that Weenah was far away in the woods, for her father Shooks-gee loved her much. But one evening there came up out of the dark pinewood forest, that lay to the north, a great band of wandering natives.

They were all armed and under the command of one of her majesty's most bloodthirsty and daring chiefs.

Hand to claw this man had fought pumas and jaguars, and slain them, armed only with his two-edged knife.

This savage Rob Roy M'Gregor despised both bow-and-arrow and sling. Only at close quarters would he fight with man or beast, and although he bore the scars and slashes of many a fearful encounter, he had always come off victorious.

Six feet four inches in height was this war-Indian if an inch, and his dress was a picturesque costume of skins with the tails attached. A huge mat of hair, his own, with emu's feathers drooping therefrom, was his only head-gear, but round his neck he wore a chain of polished pebbles, with heavy gold rings, in many of which rubies and diamonds sparkled and shone.

But, ghastly to relate, between each pebble and between the rings of gold and precious stones, was threaded a tanned human ear. More than twenty of these were there.

They had been cut from the heads of white men whom this chief—Kaloomah was his name—had slain, and the rings had been torn from their dead fingers.

This was the band then that had arrived as the sun was going down at the hut of Shooks-gee, and this was their chief.

The latter demanded food for his men, and Shooks-gee, with his trembling wife—Weenah was hidden—made haste to obey, and a great fire was lit out of doors, and flesh of the llama hung over it to roast.

But the strangest thing was this. Seated on a hardy little mule was a sad but beautiful girl—white she was, and unmistakably English. Her eyes were very large and wistful, and she looked at Kaloomah and his band in evident fear and dread, starting and shrinking from the chief whenever he came near her or spoke.

But the daintiest portion of the food was handed to her, and she ate in silence, as one will who eats in fear.

The wild band slept in the bush, a special bed of dry grass being made for the little white queen, as Kaloomah called her, and a savage set to watch her while she slept.

Next morning, when the wild chief and his braves started onwards, Shooks-gee was obliged to march along with them.

Kaloomah had need of him. That was all the explanation vouchsafed.

But this visit to the queen's home had given Weenah's father an insight into court life and usages that he could not otherwise have possessed.

Kaloomah's band bore along with them huge bales of cloth and large boxes of beads. How they had become possessed of these Shooks-gee never knew, and could not guess.

The grim and haughty queen, surrounded by her body-guard of grotesque and hideous warriors with their slashed and fearful faces, and the peleles hanging in the lobes of their ears, was seated at the farther end of a great wall, and on a throne covered with the skins of wild beasts.

All in front the floor was carpeted with crimson, and her majesty sparkled with gold ornaments. A tiara of jewels encircled her brow, and a living snake of immense size, with gray eyes that never closed, formed a girdle round her waist.

In her hand she held a poisoned spear, and at her feet crouched a huge jaguar.

She was a tyrant queen, reigning over a people who, though savage, and cannibals to boot, had never dared to gainsay a word or order she uttered.

Passionate in the extreme, too, she was, and if a slave or subject dared to disobey, a prick from the poisoned spear was the reward, and he or she was dragged out into the bush to writhe and die in terrible agony.

Probably a more frightful woman never reigned as queen, even in cannibal lands.

Kaloomah, on his arrival, bent himself down—nay, but threw himself on his knees and face abjectly before her, as if he were scarcely worthy to be her footstool.

But she greeted his arrival with a smile, and bade him arise.

"Many presents have we brought," he said in the figurative language of the Indian. "Many presents to the beautiful mother of the sun. Cloth of scarlet, of blue, and of green, cloth of rainbow colours, jewels and beads, and the fire-water of the pale-faces."

"Produce me the fire-water of the pale-faces," she returned. "I would drink."

Her voice was husky, hoarse, and horrible.

Kaloomah beckoned to a slave, and in a few minutes a cocoa-nut shell, filled with rum, was held to her lips.

The queen drank, and seemed happier after this. Kaloomah thought he might now venture to broach another subject.

"We have brought your majesty also a little daughter of the pale-faces!"

Then Peggy—for the reader will have guessed it was she—was led trembling in before her, and made to kneel.

But the queen's brows had lowered when she beheld the child's great beauty. She made her advance, and seizing her by the hand, held her at arm's-length.

*"SHE ... HELD HER AT ARM'S LENGTH"*

"Take her away!" she cried. "I can love her not. Put her in prison below ground!"

And the beautiful girl was hurried away.

To be put in prison below the ground meant to be buried alive. But Kaloomah had no intention of obeying the queen on this occasion, and the girl pale-face was conducted to a well-lighted bamboo hut and placed in charge of a woman slave.

This slave looked a heart-broken creature, but seemed kind and good, and now made haste to spread the girl's bed of leaves on a bamboo bench, and to place before her milk of the llama, with much luscious fruit and nuts. She needed little pressing to eat, or drink, or sleep. The poor child had almost ceased to wonder, or even to be afraid of anything.

But now comes the last act in Shooks-gee's strange story.

Two days after the arrival of the warlike band from the far north, Kaloomah had once more presented himself before the queen. He came unannounced this time, and with him were seven fierce-looking soldiers, armed to the teeth with slings and stones, with bows and arrows, and with spears.

The conversation that had ensued was somewhat as follows, being interpreted into our plain and humdrum English:—

*The Queen.* "Why advances my general and slave except on his knees, even as come the frogs?"

*Kaloomah.* "My queen will pardon me. I will not so offend again. Your majesty has reigned long and happily."

*Q.* "True, slave."

She seized the poisoned spear as she spoke, and would have used it freely; but at a word from Kaloomah it was wrenched from her grasp.

*K.* "Your majesty's reign has ended! The old queen must make room for the beautiful daughter of the pale-faces. Yet will your beneficence live in the person of the new queen, and in our hearts—the hearts of those who have fought for you. For we each and all shall taste of your roasted flesh!"

Then, turning quickly to the soldiers, "Seize her and drag her forth!" he cried, "and do your duty speedily."

I must not be too graphic in my description of the scene that followed. But the ex-queen was led to a darksome hut, and there she was speedily despatched.

That night high revelry was held in the royal camp of the cannibals. Many prisoners were killed and roasted, and the feast was a fearful and awful one.

But not a chief was there in all that crowd who did not partake of the flesh of his late queen, while horn trumpets blared and war tom-toms were wildly beaten.

A piece of the fearful flesh was even given to the pale-face girl's attendant, with orders that she must make her charge partake thereof.

The girl was spared this terrible ordeal, however.

But long after midnight the revelry and the wild music went on, then ceased, and all was still.

The unhappy prisoner lay listening till sleep stole down on a star-ray and wafted her off to the land of sweet forgetfulness.

---

Next day, amidst wild unearthly clamour and music, she was led from the tent and seated on the throne. Garments of otter skins and crimson cloth were cast on the throne and draped over the beautiful child. She was encircled with flowers of rarest hue, and emu's feathers were stuck, plume-like, in her bonnie hair.

Meanwhile the trumpets blared more loudly, and the tom-toms were struck with treble force, then all ceased at once, and there was a silence deep as death, as everyone prostrated himself or herself before the newly-made young queen.

Kaloomah rose at last, and advanced with bended back and head towards her, and with an intuitive sense of her new-born dignity she touched him gently on the shoulder and bade him stand erect.

He did so, and then placed in her hand the sceptre of the dead queen—the poison-tipped spear.

Whatever might happen now, the girl knew that she was safe for a time, and her spirits rose in consequence.

This, then, was the story told by Shooks-gee, the father of Benee's child-love.

---

Had Dick Temple himself been there he could no longer have doubted the fidelity of poor Benee.

But there was much to be done, and it would need all the tact and skill of this wily Indian to carry out his plans.

He could trust his father and mother, as he called Weenah's parents, and he now told them that he had come, if possible, to deliver Peggy, or if that were impossible, to hand her a letter that should give her both comfort and hope.

Queen Peggy's apartments on the mountain were cannibalistically regal in their splendour. The principal entrance to her private room was approached by a long avenue of bamboo rails, completely lined with skulls and bones, and the door thereof was also surrounded by the same kind of horrors.

But every one of her subjects was deferential to her, and appeared awestruck with her beauty.

And now Benee consulted with his parents as to what had best be done.

# CHAPTER XVI—ON THE BANKS OF A BEAUTIFUL RIVER

They would not allow Benee to harbour for a single moment the idea of stealing the queen and escaping with her into the forest.

Two thousand armed men were stationed within a mile of the camp, so Benee would speedily be killed, and in all likelihood Queen Peggy also.

No; and he must go no farther into the land of the cannibals.

But he, Shooks-gee, undertook to give the queen a little note-book, in which a letter was written from her "brother", stating that all haste was being made to come to her deliverance. He would receive back the note-book, and therein would doubtless be written poor Peggy's letter. Meanwhile Benee must wait.

Shooks-gee started on his mission next day.

He was away for a whole week, but it seemed but a few hours to Benee. He had divested himself of his arms, and given the cloth and beads to Weenah's mother. Then all the dear old life of his boyhood seemed to be renewed. Weenah and he wandered wild and free once more in the forest and over the heath-clad plains; they fished in lake and stream; they ate and drank together under the shade of the pine-tree, and listened to the love-song of the sweet soo-soo.

It was all like a happy, happy dream. And is not the love-life of the young always a dream of bliss? Ah! but it is one from which there is ever an awakening.

And with the return of Shooks-gee, Benee's dream came to an end.

Peggy had written her long, sad story in the notebook.

Benee knew it was long, but he could not read it.

Then farewells were said.

The child Weenah clung to Benee's neck and wept. She thought she could not let him go, and at last he had to gently tear himself away and disappear speedily in the forest.

Just one glance back at Weenah's sad and wistful face, then the jungle swallowed him up, and he would be seen by Weenah, mayhap, never again.

----------

It was not without considerable misgivings that Roland and Dick Temple made a start for the country of the cannibals.

The relief party consisted but of one hundred white men all told, with about double that number of carriers. It was, of course, the first real experience of these boys on the war-path, and difficulty after difficulty presented itself, but was bravely met and overcome.

"Uneasy lies the head that wears a crown."

Probably the general of an army, be it of what size it may, is more to be pitied than even a king. The latter has his courtiers and his parliament to advise him; the general is *princeps*, he is chief, and has only his own skill and judgment to fall back upon.

It had been suggested by Burly Bill that instead of journeying overland as a first start, and having to cross the whirling river Purus and many lesser streams before striking the Madeira some distance above the Amazon, they should drop down-stream in steamer-loads, and assemble at the junction of the former with the latter.

Neither Roland nor Dick thought well of the plan, and herein lay their first mistake. Not only was it weeks before they were able to reach the Madeira, but they had the grief of losing one white man and one Indian with baggage in the crossing of the Purus.

We cannot put old heads on young shoulders; nevertheless the wise youth never fails to profit by the experience of his elders.

132

Even when they reached the forest lands on the west side of the Madeira, another long delay ensued. For here they had to encamp on somewhat damp and unwholesome ground until Burly Bill should descend the stream to hire canoes or boats suitable for passing the rapids.

Don Pedro or Peter was now doing his best to make himself agreeable. He was laughing and singing all day long, but this fact in no way deceived Roland, and as a special precaution he told off several white men to act as detectives and to be near him by day and by night.

If Peter were really the blood-guilty wretch that Roland, if not Dick, believed him to be, he made one mistake now. He tried his very utmost to make friends with Brawn, the great Irish wolf-hound, but was, of course, unsuccessful.

"I sha'n't take bite nor sup from that evil man's hand," Brawn seemed to say to himself. "He looks as if he would poison me. But," he added, "he shall have my undivided attention at night."

And so this huge hound guarded Peter, never being ten yards away from the man's sleeping-skin till up leapt the sun in the gold and crimson east and shone on the waters of the beautiful river.

"That dog is getting very fond of you, I think," said Roland one day to Peter, while Brawn was snuffing his hand. "You see how well he protects you by night. He will never lie near to either Dick or me."

Peter replied in words that were hardly audible, but were understood to mean that he was obliged to Brawn for his condescension. But he somewhat marred the beauty of his reply by adding a swear-word or two at the end.

While they waited in camp here for the return of Bill and his crews, they went in for sport of several sorts.

The fish in this river are somewhat remarkable—remarkable alike for their numbers and for their appearance—but all are not edible.

"How are we to know, I wonder, which we should cook and which we shouldn't?" said Roland to his friend, Dick Temple.

"I think," replied Dick, "that we may safely cook any of them, but, as to eating, why, I should only eat those that are nice in flavour."

"That's right. We'll be guided by that rule."

The boys fished from canoes which they hired or requisitioned from the Indian natives of the place. Clever these fellows are, and the manner in which they watch for and harpoon or even spear a huge "boto"—which looks like a long-snouted porpoise or "sea-pig"—astonished our heroes.

This fish is killed by whites only for its oil, but the Indians did not hesitate to cut huge fourteen-pound pieces from the back to take home for culinary purposes.

The "piraroocoo" is an immense fellow, and calculated to give good sport for a long summer day if you do not know how to handle him.

This "'roocoo", as some of the natives call him, likes to hang around in the back reaches of the river, and is often found ten feet in length.

He has the greatest objection in the world to being caught, and to being killed after being dragged on shore. Moreover, he has a neat and very expert way of lifting a canoe on his back for a few seconds, and letting it down bottom-upwards.

When he does so, you, the sportsman or piscador, find yourself floundering in the water. You probably gulp down about half a gallon of river water, but you thank your stars you learned to swim when a boy, and strike out for the bank. But five to one you have a race to run with an intelligent 'gator. If he is hungry, you may as well think about some short prayer to say; if he is not very ravenous, you may win just by a neck.

This last was an experience of Dick's one day; when a 'roocoo capsized his frail canoe and his Indian and he got spilt.

Luckily Roland was on the beach, and just as a huge 'gator came ploughing up behind poor Dick, with head and awful jaws above water,

Roland took steady aim and fired. Then the creature turned on his back, and the river was dyed with blood.

The natives salt the 'roocoo and eat it. But Roland's Indian carriers managed to get through as many as could be caught, without any salt worth speaking about.

Surely the fish in this beautiful river must have thought it strange, that so many of their number were constantly disappearing heavenwards at the end of a line. But it did not trouble them very much after all, and they learnt no lesson from what they saw, but took the bait as readily as ever.

There were very many other species of fish, which not only gave good sport but made a most delicious *addendum* to the larder.

Boats and canoes were now in the river all day long, and with the fish caught, and the turtle which were found in great abundance, not to mention the wild animals killed in the woods, Roland managed to feed his little army well.

There is one fish in this river which is sometimes called "diabolo". He is no relation at all, however, to the real octopus or devil-fish, for this creature is flat. It seems a species of ray, and has an immense mouthful of the very sharpest of teeth. He is not at all dainty as to what he eats. He can make a meal off fresh-water shell-fish; he can swallow his smaller brothers of the deep; take a snack from a dead 'gator, and is quite at home while discussing a nice tender one-pound steak from a native's leg.

The young 'gator is neither fish, flesh, nor good red-herring. Yet if you catch one not over a yard long, and he doesn't catch you—for he has a wicked way of seizing a man by the hand and holding on till his mother comes,—his tail, stewed or fried with a morsel of pork, will tide you over a "hungry hillock" very pleasantly indeed.

If we turn to the pleasant reaches of the River Madeira, or the quiet back-waters, and, gun on shoulder, creep warily through the bush and scrub, we shall be rewarded with a sight that will well repay our caution.

Here of an early morning we shall see water-fowl innumerable, and of the greatest beauty imaginable.

Hidden from view, one is loth indeed to fire a shot and so disturb Nature's harmony, but prefers, for a time at all events, to crouch there quietly and watch the strange antics of the male birds and the meek docility of the female.

Here are teal, black ducks, strange wild geese, brown ducks, sheldrakes, widgeons, and whatnot.

And yonder on the shore, in all sorts of droll attitudes with their ridiculously long necks and legs, are storks and herons. I think they like to perform their toilet close to the calm pellucid water, because it serves the same purpose to them as a bedroom mirror does to us.

Young tapirs form a welcome addition to the larder, and the woods all round abound in game.

What a paradise! and yet this country is hardly yet known to us young Britons. We hear of ague. Bah! Regularity of living, and a dust of quinine, and camping in the open, can keep fever of all sorts at bay.

Some may be surprised that our heroes should have settled down, as it were, so enthusiastically to fishing and sporting, although uncertain all the while as to the fate of poor kidnapped Peggy.

True, but we must remember that activity and constant employment are the only cure for grief. So long, then, as Roland and Dick were busy with gun or fishing-rod, they were free from thought and care.

But after sunset, when the long dark night closed over the camp; when the fire-flies danced from bush to bush, and all was still save the wind that sighed among the trees, or the voices of night-birds and prowling beasts, and the rush of the river fell on the ear in drowsy, dreamy monotone, then the boys felt their anxiety acutely enough, but bravely tried to give each other courage, and their conversation, oft-repeated, was somewhat as follows:—

*Roland.* "You're a bit gloomy to-night, Dick, I think?"

*Dick.* "Well, Roll, the night is so pitchy dark, never a moon, and only a star peeping out now and then. Besides I am thinking of—"

*Roland.* "Hush! hush! aren't we both always thinking about her? Though I won't hesitate to say it is wrong not to be hopeful and cheerful."

*Dick.* "But do you believe—"

*Roland.* "I believe this, Dick, that if those kidnapping revengeful Indians had meant murder they would have slain the dear child in bed and not have resorted to all that horrible trickery—instigated without doubt by somebody. She has been taken to the country of the cannibals, but not to be tortured. She is a slave, let us hope, to some Indian princess, and well-guarded too. What we have got to do is to trust in God. I'm no preacher, but that is so. And we've got to do our duty and rescue Peggy."

*Dick.* "Dead or alive, Roland."

*Roland.* "Dead or alive, Dick. But Heaven have mercy on the souls of those who harm a hair of her head!"

———

Dick did his best to trust in Providence, but often in the middle watches of the night he would lie in his tent thinking, thinking, and unable to sleep; then, after perhaps an uneasy slumber towards morning, awake somewhat wearily to resume the duties of the day.

# CHAPTER XVII—BILL AND HIS BOATS

Roland, young and inexperienced as he was, proved himself a fairly good general.

He certainly had not forgotten the salt, nor anything else that was likely to add to the comfort of his people in this very long cruise by river and by land.

They knew not what was before them, nor what trouble or dangers they might have to encounter, so our young heroes were pretty well prepared to fight or to rough it in every way.

Independent of very large quantities of ammunition for rifles and revolvers, Roland had prepared a quantity of war-rockets, for nothing strikes greater terror into the breasts of the ordinary savage than these fire-devils, as they term them.

Roland, Dick, and Bill each had shot-guns, with sheath-knives, and a sort of a portable bill-hook, which many of the men carried also, and found extremely handy for making a clearance among reeds, rushes, or lighter bush.

We have already seen that they had plenty of fishing-tackle.

Oil and pumice-stone were not forgotten, and Roland had a regular inspection of his men every day, to make certain that their rifles and revolvers were clean.

But this was not all, for, to the best of their ability, both Roland and Dick drilled their men to the use of their arms at short and long distances, and taught them to advance and retire in skirmishing order, taking advantage of every morsel of cover which the ground might afford.

Plenty of maize and corn-flour were carried, and quite a large supply of tinned provisions, from the plantation and from Burnley Hall. These included canned meat, sardines, and salmon.

Extra clothing was duly arranged for, because from the plains they would have to ascend quite into the regions of cloud and storm, if not snow.

Medicine, too, but only a very little of this, Roland thought, would be needed, although, on the other hand, he stowed away lint and bandages in abundance, with a few surgical instruments.

Medical comforts? Yes, and these were not to be considered as luxuries, though they took the form of brandy and good wine.

Good tea, coffee, cocoa, and coca were, of course, carried, with sugar to sweeten these luxuries.

But a small cask of fire-water—arrack—was included among the stores, and this was meant as a treat for native Indians, if they should happen to meet any civil and obliging enough to hobnob.

Money would be of no use in the extreme wilds. Salt, and cloth of gaudy colours, to say nothing of beads, would be bartered for articles of necessity.

————————

Everything was ready for the start, but still there were no signs of Bill and the boats.

It was the first question Roland asked Dick of a morning, or Dick asked Roland, according to who happened to be first up:

"Any signs of Bill and the boats?"

"None!"

On the top of a cliff at the bend of the beautiful river stood a very tall tree, and right on top of this was an outlook—an Indian boy, who stayed two hours on watch, and was then relieved.

He could command quite an extensive view downstream, and was frequently hailed during the day and asked about Bill and his boats, but the answer would come somewhat dolefully:

"Plenty boat, sah, but no Beel."

Yes, there were boats of many kinds, and a few steamers now and then also, but Roland held no intercourse with any of these. His little army was encamped on an open clearing well back in the forest. He did not wish to know anyone's business, and he determined that his own should not leak out.

But although Roland and Dick had plenty to do, and there was sport enough to be had, still the time began to drag wearily on day by day, and both young fellows were burning for action and movement and "go".

Peter, *alias* Don Pedro, seemed as anxious as anyone else to get forward.

He was most quiet and affable to everyone, although apt to drop into dejected moods at times.

He saw that he was not wholly in bad favour with Dick Temple.

One day, when Roland was at the other side of the river, after smoking in silence for some time by the banks of the stream, where, in company with Dick and Brawn, he was sitting, a down-steamer hove in sight at the bend of the river, and both waved their caps to those on board, a salute which was cheerfully returned.

The vessel was some distance out in the broad river, but presently Dick could see a huge black-board held over the port-quarter. There was writing in chalk on it, and Dick speedily put his lorgnettes up, and read as follows:—

IF GOING UP RIVER—BEWARE!

KARAPOONA SAVAGES ON WAR-PATH—TREACHERY!


"Forewarned is forearmed!" said Dick.

"What was the legend exposed to view on the telegraph board?" asked Peter languidly.

"The Karapoona savages on the war-path," replied Dick.

"What! The Karapoonas! A fearful race, and cannibals to boot—"

"You know them then?"

"What, I? I—I—no—no, only what I have heard."

He took three or four whiffs of his cigarette in quick succession, as if afraid of its going dead.

But Dick's eye was on him all the time.

He seemed not to care to meet it.

"Bound for Pará, no doubt," he said at last. "I do wish I were on board."

"No doubt, Mr. Peter, and really we seem to be taking you on this expedition somewhat against your will?"

"True; and I am a man of the world, and have not failed to notice that I am in some measure under the ban of suspicion.

"Yet, I think you are not unfriendly to me," he added.

"No, Mr. Peter, I am unfriendly to no one."

"Then, might you not use your influence with your friend, Mr. St. Clair, to let me catch the first boat back to Pará?"

"I cannot interfere with Mr. Roland St. Clair's private concerns. If he suspects you of anything in the shape of duplicity or treachery and you are innocent, you have really nothing to fear. As to letting you off your engagement, that is his business. I can only say that the tenure of your office is not yet complete, and that you are his head-clerk for still another year."

"True, true, but I came as governor of the estate, and not to accompany a mad-cap expedition like this. Besides, Mr. Temple, I am far from strong. I am a man of peace, too, and have hardly ever fired a revolver in my life.

"But I have another very urgent reason for getting back to England—"

"No doubt, Mr. Peter!"

This was almost a sneer.

"No doubt—but I interrupt you."

"My other reason may appeal to you in more ways than one. I am in love, Mr. Temple—"

"You!"

"I am in love, and engaged to be married to one of the sweetest girls in Cornwall. If I am detained here, and unable to write, she may think me dead —and—and—well, anything might happen."

"Pah, Mr. Peter! I won't say I don't believe you, but instead of your little romance appealing to me, it simply disgusts me. I tell you straight, sir, you don't look like a man to fall in love with anything except gold; but if the young lady is really fond of you, she will lose neither hope nor heart, even if she does not hear of you or from you for a year or more."

Then, seeing that he seemed to wound this strange man's feelings:

"Pardon my brusqueness, Mr. Peter," he added more kindly. "I really do not mean to hurt you. Come, cheer up, and if I can help you—I will."

Peter held out his hand.

Dick simply touched it.

He could not get himself even to like the man.

———————

The signal-tree was but a few yards distant from the spot where they sat.

And now there came a wild, excited hail therefrom.

"Golly foh true, Massa Dick!"

Brawn jumped up, and barked wildly.

His echo came from beyond the stream, and he barked still more wildly at that.

"Well, boy," shouted Dick, "do you see anything?"

"Plenty moochee see. Beel come. Not very far off. Beel and de boats!"

This was indeed joyful news for Dick. He happened to glance at Peter for a moment, however, and could not help being struck with the change that seemed to have come over him. He appeared to have aged suddenly. His face was gray, his lips compressed, his brows lowered and stern.

Dick never forgot that look.

Dick Temple was really good-hearted, and he felt for this man, and something kept telling him he was innocent and wronged.

But he had nothing to fear if innocent. He would certainly be put to inconvenience, but for that, if all went well, Roland would not fail to recompense him handsomely, and he—Dick—had a duty to perform to his friend. So now in the bustle that followed—if Peter wanted to make a rush for the woods—he might try.

Roland had heard the hail, and his canoe was now coming swiftly on towards the bank. Dick ran to meet him.

When he half-pulled his friend on shore and turned back with him, behold! Peter was gone.

# CHAPTER XVIII—AS IF STRUCK BY A DUM-DUM BULLET

Roland and Dick walked quickly towards the camp.

It was all a scene of bustle and stir indescribable, for good news as well as bad travels apace.

"Bill and the boats are coming!" Englishmen were shouting.

"Beel and de boats!" chorused the Indians.

But on the approach of "the young captains", as the boys were called, comparative peace was restored.

"Had anyone seen Mr. Peter?" was the first question put by our heroes to their white officers. "No," from all.

"He had disappeared for a few moments in his tent," said an Indian, "then der was no more Massa Peter."

Scouts and armed runners were now speedily got together, and Roland gave them orders. They were to search the bush and forest, making a long detour or outflanking movement, then closing round a centre, as if in battue, to allow not a tree to go unexamined.

This was all that could be done.

So our heroes retraced their steps towards the river bank, where, lo! they beheld a whole fleet of strange canoes, big and small, being rowed swiftly towards them.

In the bows of the biggest—a twelve-tonner—stood Burly Bill himself.

He was blacker with the sun than ever, and wildly waving the broadest kind of Panama hat ever seen on the Madeira. But in his left hand he clutched his meerschaum, and such clouds was he blowing that one might have mistaken the great canoe for a steam-launch.

He jumped on shore as soon as the prow touched the bank—the water here being deep.

Black though Burly Bill was, his smile was so pleasant, and his face so good-natured, that everybody who looked at him felt at once on excellent terms with himself and with all created things.

"I suppose I ought to apologize, Mr. Roland, for the delay—I—"

"And I suppose," interrupted Roland, "you ought to do nothing of the kind. Dinner is all ready, Bill; come and eat first. Put guards in your boats, and march along. Your boys will be fed immediately."

It was a splendid dinner.

Burly Bill, who was more emphatic than choice in English, called it a tiptopper, and all hands in Roland's spacious tent did ample justice to it.

Roland even spliced the main-brace, as far as Bill was concerned, by opening a bottle of choice port.

The boys themselves merely sipped a little. What need have lads under twenty for vinous stimulants?

Bill's story was a long one, but I shall not repeat it. He had encountered the greatest difficulty imaginable in procuring the sort of boats he needed.

"But," he added, "all's well that end's well, I guess, and we'll start soon now, I suppose, for the rapids of Antonio."

"Yes," said Roland, "we'll strike camp possibly to-morrow; but we must do as much loading up as possible to-night."

"That's the style," said Bill. "We've got to make haste. Only we've got to think! 'Haste but not hurry', that's my motto.

"But I say," he continued, "I miss two friends—where is Mr. Peter and where is Brawn?"

"Peter has taken French leave, I fear, and Brawn, where is Brawn, Dick?"

"I really did not miss either till now," answered Dick, "but let us continue to be fair to Mr. Peter— Listen!"

At that moment shouting was heard far down the forest.

The noise came nearer and nearer, and our heroes waited patiently.

In five minutes' time into the tent bounded the great wolf-hound, gasping but laughing all down both sides, and with about a foot of pink tongue—more or less—hanging out at one side, over his alabaster teeth.

He quickly licked Roland's ears and Dick's, then uttered one joyous bark and made straight for Burly Bill.

Yes, Bill was burly, but Brawn fairly rolled him over and nearly smothered him with canine caresses. Then he took a leap back to the boys as much as to say:

"Why don't you rejoice too? Wouff—wouff! Aren't you glad that Bill has returned? Wouff! What would life be worth anyhow without Bill? Wouff —wouff—wow!"

But the last wow ended in a low growl, as Peter himself stood smiling at the opening.

"Why, Mr. Peter, we thought you were lost!" cried Dick.

Mr. Peter walked up to Bill and shook hands.

"Glad indeed to see you back," he said nonchalantly, "and you're not looking a bit paler. Any chance of a morsel to eat?"

"Sit down," cried Dick. "Steward!"

"Yes, sah; to be surely, sah. Dinner foh Massa Peter? One moment, sah."

Mr. Peter was laughing now, but he had seated himself on the withered grass as far as possible from Brawn.

"I must say that three hours in a tree-top gives one the devil's own appetite," he began. "I had gone to take a stroll in the forest, you know—"

"Yes," said Roland, "we do know."

Mr. Peter looked a little crestfallen, but said pointedly enough: "If you do know, there is no need for me to tell you."

"Oh, yes, go on!" cried Dick.

"Well then, I had not gone half a mile, and was just lighting up a cigarette, when Brawn came down on me, and I had barely time to spring into the tree before he reached the foot of it. There I waited as patiently as Job would have done—thank you, steward, what a splendid Irish stew!—till by and by—a precious long by and by—your boys came to look for Brawn, and in finding Brawn they found poor famishing me. Thank you, Bill, I'll be glad of a little wine."

"Looking for Brawn, they found you, eh!" said Roland. "I should have put it differ—"

But Dick punched Roland's leg, and Roland laughed and said no more.

———

Two days after the arrival of Burly Bill an order was given for general embarkation. All under their several officers were inspected on the river bank, and to each group was allotted a station in boat or canoe.

The head men or captains from whom Bill had hired the transport were in every instance retained, but a large number of Roland's own Indians were most expert rowers, and therefore to take others would only serve to load the vessels uncomfortably, not to say dangerously.

But peons or paddlers to the number of two or four to each large canoe their several captains insisted on having.

The inspection on the bank was a kind of "muster by open list", and Roland was exceedingly pleased with the result, for not a man or boy was missing.

It was a delightful day when the expedition was at last got under way.

Roland and Dick, with Peter, to say nothing of Brawn, occupied the after-cabin in a canoe of very light draught, but really a twelve-tonner. The cabin was, of course, both dining-room and sleeping berth—the lounges being skins of buffaloes and of wild beasts, but all clean and sweet.

The cabin itself was built of bamboo and bamboo leaves lined with very light skins, so overlapping as to make the cabin perfectly dry.

Our heroes had arranged about light, and candles were brought out as soon as daylight began to fade.

Then the canoes were paddled towards the bank or into some beautiful reach or back-water, and there made fast for the night with padlock and chain.

Roland and Dick had their own reasons for taking such strict precautions.

The first day passed without a single adventure worth relating.

The paddlers or peons, of whom there were seven on each side of our hero's huge canoe, worked together well. They oftentimes sang or chanted a wild indescribable kind of boat-lilt, to which the sound of the paddles was an excellent accompaniment, but now and then the captain would shout: "Choorka—choorka!" which, from the excitement the words caused, evidently meant "Sweep her up!" and then the vessel seemed to fly over the water and dance in the air.

Other canoe captains would take up the cry, and "Choorka—Choorka!" would resound from every side.

A sort of race was on at such times, but the *Burnley Hall*, as Roland's boat was called, nearly always left the others astern.

Dinner was cooked on shore, and nearly everyone landed at night. Only our heroes stuck to their boat.

There were moon and stars at present, and very pleasant it was to sit, or rather lie, at their open-sided cabin, and to watch these mirrored in the calm water, while fire-flies danced and flitted from bush to bush.

But there was always the sorrow and the weight of grief lying deep down in the hearts of both Roland and Dick; the ever-abiding anxiety, the one question they kept asking themselves constantly, and which could not be answered, "Shall we be in time to save poor Peggy?"

Mr. Peter slept on shore.

Brawn kept him company. Kept untiring watch over him. And two faithful and well-armed Indians lay in the bush at a convenient distance.

In a previous chapter I have mentioned an ex-cannibal Bolivian, whom Roland had made up his mind to take with him as a guide in the absence of, or in addition to, faithful Benee.

He was called Charlie by the whites.

Charlie was as true to his master as the needle to the pole.

On the third evening of the voyage, just as Roland and Dick, with Bill, were enjoying an after-dinner lounge in an open glade not far from the river brink, the moon shining so brightly that the smallest of type could easily have been read by young eyes, he suddenly appeared in their midst.

"What cheer, Charlie?" said Roland kindly. "Come, squat thee down, and we will give you a tiny toothful of aguardiente."

"Touchee me he, no, no!" was the reply. "He catchee de bref too muchee. Smokee me, notwidstanding," he added.

It was one of Charlie's peculiarities that if he could once get hold of a big word or two, he planted them in his conversation whenever he thought he had a favourable opening.

An ex-cannibal Charlie was, and he came from the great western unexplored district of Bolivia.

He confessed that although fond of "de pig ob de forest (tapir), de tail ob de 'gator, and de big haboo-snake when roast," there was nothing in all the world so satisfactory as "de fles' ob a small boy. Yum, yum! it was goodee, goodee notwidstanding, and make bof him ear crack and him 'tumack feel wa'm."

Charlie lit up his cigarette, and then commenced to explain the reason of his visit.

"What you callee dat?" he said, handing Burly Bill a few large purple berries of a species of thorny laurel.

"Why," said Bill, "these are the fruit of the lanton-tree, used for poisoning arrow-tips."

"And dis, sah. What you callee he? Mind, mind, no touchee de point! He poison, notwidstanding."

It was a thin bamboo cane tipped with a fine-pointed nail.

Bill waited for him to explain.

He condescended to do so at last.

"Long time ago I runee away from de cannibal Indians notwidstanding. I young den, I fat, I sweet in flesh. Sometime my leg look so nice, I like to eat one little piecee ob myse'f. But no. Charlie not one big fool. But de chief tink he like me. He take me to him tent one day, den all muchee quickee he slaves run in and take up knife. Ha, ha! I catchee knife too, notwidstanding. Charlie young and goodee and plenty mooch blood fly.

"I killee dat chief, and killee bof slaves. Den I runned away.

"Long time I wander in de bush, but one day I come to de tents ob de white men. Dey kind to poh Charlie, and gib me work. I lub de white man; all same, I no lub Massa Peter."

He paused to puff at a fresh cigarette.

"And," he added, "I fine dat poison berry and dat leetle poison spear in place where Massa Peter sleep."

"Ho, ho!" said Bill.

Charlie grew a little more excited as he continued: "As shuah as God madee me, de debbil hisself makee dat bad man Peter. He wantee killee poh Brawn. Dat what for, notwidstanding."

Now although there be some human beings—they are really not worth the name—who hate dogs, every good-hearted man or woman in the world loves those noble animals who are, next to man, the best and bravest that God has created.

But there are degrees in the love people bear for their pets. If a faithful dog like Brawn is constantly with one, he so wins one's affection that death alone can sever the tie.

Not only Roland, but Dick also, dearly loved Brawn, and the bare idea that he was in danger of his life so angered both that, had Mr. Peter been present when honest Charlie the Indian made his communication, one of them would most certainly have gone for him in true Etonian style, and the man would have been hardly presentable at court for a fortnight after at the least.

"Dick," said Roland, the red blood mounting to his brow, the fire seeming to scintillate from his eyes. "Dick, old man, what do you advise?"

"I know what I should like to do," answered Dick, with clenched fist and lowered brows.

"So do I, Dick; but that might only make matters worse.

"But Heaven keep me calm, old man," he continued, "for now I shall send for Peter and have it out with him. Not at present, you say? But, Dick, I am all on fire. I must, I shall speak to him. Charlie, retire; I would not have Mr. Peter taking revenge on so good a fellow as you."

At Dick's earnest request Roland waited for half an hour before he sent for Peter.

This gentleman advanced from the camp fire humming an operatic air, and with a cigar in hand.

"Oh, Mr. Peter," said Roland, "I was walking near your sleeping place of last night and picked this up."

He held up the little bamboo spear.

"What is it?" said Peter. "An arrow? I suppose some of the Indians dropped it. I never saw it before. It seems of little consequence," he continued, "though I dare say it would suffice to pink a rat with."

He laughed lightly as he spoke. "Was this all you wanted me for, Mr. St. Clair?"

He was handling the little spear as he spoke. Next moment:

"Merciful Father!" he suddenly screamed, "I have pricked myself! I am poisoned! I am a dead man! Brandy— Oh, quick— Oh—!"

He said never a word more, but dropped on the moss as if struck by a dum-dum bullet.

And there he lay, writhing in torture, foaming at the mouth, from which blood issued from a bitten tongue.

It was a ghastly and horrible sight. Roland looked at Dick.

"Dick," he said, "the man knew it was poisoned."

"Better he should die than Brawn."

"Infinitely," said Roland.

# CHAPTER XIX—STRUGGLING ONWARDS UP-STREAM

"But," said Roland, "it would be a pity to let even Peter die, as we may have need of him. Let us send for Charlie at once. Perhaps he can tell us of an antidote."

The Indian was not far off.

"Fire-water", was his reply to Dick's question, "and dis."

"Dis" was the contents of a tiny bottle, which he speedily rubbed into the wound in Peter's hand.

The steward, as one of the men was called, quickly brought a whole bottle of rum, the poisoned man's jaws were forced open, and he was literally drenched with the hot and fiery spirit.

But spasm after spasm took place after this, and while the body was drawn up with cramp, and the muscles knotted and hard, the features were fearfully contorted.

By Roland's directions chloroform was now poured on a handkerchief, and after this was breathed by the sufferer for a few minutes the muscles became relaxed, and the face, though still pale as death, became more sightly.

More rum and more rubbing with the antidote, and Mr. Peter slept in peace.

About sunrise he awoke, cold and shivering, but sensible.

After a little more stimulant he began to talk.

"Bitten by a snake, have I not been?"

"Mr. Peter," said Roland sternly, "you have narrowly escaped the death you would have meted out to poor Brawn with your cruel and accursed arrow.

"You may not love the dog. He certainly does not love you, and dogs are good judges of character. He tree'd you, and you sought revenge. You doubtless have other reasons to hate Brawn, but his life is far more to us than yours. Now confess you meant to do for him, and then to make your way down-stream by stealing a canoe."

"I do not, will not confess," cried Peter. "It is a lie. I am here against my will. I am kidnapped. I am a prisoner. The laws of even this country—and sorry I am ever I saw it—will and shall protect me."

Roland was very calm, even to seeming carelessness.

"We are on the war-path at present, my friend," he said very quietly. "You are suspected of one of the most horrible crimes that felon ever perpetrated, that of procuring the abduction of Miss St. Clair and handing her over to savages."

"As Heaven is above us," cried Peter, "I am guiltless of that!"

"Hush!" roared Roland, "why take the sacred name of Heaven within your vile lips. Were you not about to die, I would strike you where you stand."

"To die, Mr. Roland? You—you—you surely don't mean—"

Roland placed a whistle to his lips, and its sound brought six stern men to his side.

"Bind that man's hands behind his back and hang him to yonder tree," was the order.

In two minutes' time the man was pinioned and the noose dangling over his head.

As he stood there, arrayed but in shirt and trousers, pale and trembling, with the cold sweat on his brow, it would have been difficult even to imagine a more distressing and pitiable sight.

His teeth chattered in his head, and he swayed about as if every moment

154

about to fall.

A man advanced, and was about to place the noose around his neck when:

"A moment, one little moment!" cried Peter. "Sir—Mr. St. Clair—I did mean to take your favourite dog's life."

"And Miss St. Clair?"

"I am innocent. If—I am to be lynched—for—that—you have the blood of a guiltless man on your head."

Dick Temple had seen enough. He advanced now to Peter's side.

"Your crime deserves lynching," he said, "but I will intercede for you if you promise me sacredly you will never attempt revenge again. If you do, as sure as fate you shall swing."

"I promise—Oh—I promise!"

Dick retired, and after a few minutes' conversation with Roland, the wretched man was set free.

*Entre nous*, reader, Roland had never really meant to lynch the man. But so utterly nerveless and broken-down was Mr. Peter now, that as soon as he was released he threw himself on the ground, crying like a child.

Even Brawn pitied him, and ran forward and actually licked the hands of the man who would have cruelly done him to death.

So noble is the nature of our friend the dog.

————

The voyage up-stream was now continued. But the progress of so many boats and men was necessarily slow, for all had to be provided for, and this meant spending about every alternate day in shooting, fishing, and collecting fruit and nuts.

The farther up-stream they got, however, the more lightsome and cheerful became the hearts of our heroes.

They began to look upon Peggy as already safe in their camp.

"I say, you know," said Dick one day, "our passage up is all toil and trouble, but won't it be delightful coming back."

"Yes, indeed," said Roland, smiling.

"We sha'n't hurry, shall we?"

"Oh, no! poor Peggy's health must need renovating, and we must let her see all that is to be seen."

"Ye—es, of course! Certainly, Roll, and it will be all just too lovely for anything, all one deliciously delicious picnic."

"I hope so."

"Don't look quite so gloomy, Roland, old man. I tell you it is all plain sailing now. We have only to meet Benee when we get as far as the rendezvous, then strike across country, and off and away to the land of the cannibals and give them fits."

"Oh, I'm not gloomy, you know, Dick, though not quite so hopeful as you! We have many difficulties to encounter, and there may be a lot of fighting after we get there; and, mind you, that game of giving fits is one that two can play at."

"Choorka! Choorka!" shouted the captain of the leading boat, a swarthy son of the river.

As he spoke, he pointed towards the western bank, and thither as quickly as paddles could send him his boat was hurried. For they had been well out in the centre of the river, and had reached a place where the current was strong and swift.

But closer to the bank it was more easy to row.

Nevertheless, two of the canoes ran foul of a snag. One was capsized at once, and the other stuck on top.

The 'gators here were in dozens apparently, and before the canoe could be righted two men had been dragged below, the brown stream being tinged with their gushing blood.

Both were Indians, but nevertheless their sad death cast a gloom over the hearts of everyone, which was not easily dispelled.

On again once more, still hugging the shore; but after dinner it was determined to stay where they were for the night.

They luckily found a fine open back-water, and this they entered and were soon snug enough.

They could not be idle, however. Food must be collected, and everything —Roland determined—must go on like clock-work, without hurry or bustle.

Soon, therefore, after the canoes were made fast, both Indians and whites were scattered far and near in the forest, on the rocks and hills, and on the rivers.

I believe that all loved the "boys", as Roland and Dick were called by the white men, and so all worked right cheerfully, laughing and singing as they did so.

Ten men besides our heroes and Burly Bill had remained behind to get the tents up and to prepare the evening meal, for everybody would return as hungry as alligators, and these gentry seem to have a most insatiable appetite.

Just before sunset on this particular evening Roland and Dick had another interview with Mr. Peter.

"I should be a fool and a fraud, Mr. Peter," said the former, "were I to mince matters. Besides, it is not my way. I tell you, then, that during our journey you will have yonder little tent to yourself to eat and to sleep in. I tell you, too, that despite your declarations of innocence I still suspect you, that nevertheless no one will be more happy than Mr. Temple here and myself if you are found not guilty. But you must face the music now. You must be guarded, strictly guarded, and I wish you to know that you are. I wish to impress upon you also that your sentries have strict orders to shoot you if you are found making any insane attempt to escape. In all other respects you are a free man, and I should be very sorry indeed to rope or tie you. Now you may go."

"My time will come," said Mr. Peter meaningly.

His face was set and determined.

"Is this a threat?" cried Roland, fingering his revolver.

But Peter's dark countenance relaxed at once.

"A threat!" he said. "No, no, Mr. Roland. I am an unarmed man, you are armed, and everyone is on your side. But I repeat, my time will come to clear my character; that is all.

"So be it, Mr. Peter."

And the man retired to his tent breathing black curses deep though not aloud.

"I've had enough of this," he told himself. "And escape that young cub's tyranny I must and shall, even should I die in my tracks. Curse them all!"

———————

Next day a deal of towing was required, for the river was running fierce and strong, and swirling in angry eddies and dangerous maelstroms even close to the bank.

This towing was tiresome work, and although all hands bent to it, half a mile an hour was their highest record.

But now they neared the terrible rapids of Antonio, and once more a halt was called for the night, in order that all might be fresh and strong to negotiate these torrents.

Next day they set to work.

All the cargo had to be got on shore, and a few armed men were left to guard it. Then the empty boats were towed up.

For three or four miles the river dashed onward here over its rocky bed, with a noise like distant thunder, a chafing, boiling, angry stream, which but to look at caused the eyes to swim and the senses to reel.

There are stretches of comparatively calm water between the rapids, and glad indeed were Roland's brave fellows to reach these for a breathing-spell.

In the afternoon, before they were half-way through these torrents, a halt was called for the night in a little bay, and the baggage was brought up.

They fell asleep that night with the roar of the rapids in their ears, and the dreams of many of them were far indeed from pleasant.

Morning brought renewal of toil and struggle. But "stout hearts to stey braes" is an excellent old Scottish motto. It was acted on by this gallant expedition, and so in a day or two they found themselves in a fresh turmoil of water beneath the splendid waterfalls of Theotonia.

The river was low, and in consequence the cataract was seen at its best, though not its maddest. Fancy, if you can, paddling to keep your way—not to advance—face to face with a waterfall a mile at least in breadth, and probably forty feet in height, divided into three by rocky little islands, pouring in white-brown sheets sheer down over the rock, and falling with a steady roar into the awful cauldrons beneath. It is like a small Niagara, but, with the hills and rocks and stately woods, and the knowledge that one is in an uncivilized land, among wild beasts and wilder men, far more impressive.

Our young heroes were astonished to note the multitudes of fish of various kinds on all sides of them. The pools were full.

The larger could be easily speared, but bait of any kind they did not seem to fancy. They were troubled and excited, for up the great stream and through the wild rapids they had made their way in order to spawn in the head-waters of the Madeira and its tributaries. But Nature here had erected a barrier.

Yet wild were their attempts to fling themselves over. Many succeeded.

The fittest would survive. Others missed, or, gaining but the rim of the cataract, were hurled back, many being killed.

Another halt, another night of dreaming of all kinds of wild adventures. The Indians had told the whites, the evening before, strange legends about the deep, almost bottomless, pools beneath the falls.

Down there, according to them, devils dwell, and hold high revelry every time the moon is full. Dark? No it is not dark at the bottom, for Indians who have been dragged down there and afterwards escaped, have related their adventures, and spoken of the splendid caverns lit up by crimson fire, whose mouths open into the water. Caverns more gorgeous and beautiful than eyes of men ever alight upon above-ground. Caverns of crystal, of jasper, onyx, and ruby; caverns around whose stalactites demons, in the form of six-legged snakes, writhe and crawl, but are nevertheless possessed of the power to change their shapes in the twinkling of an eye from the horrible and grotesque to the beautiful.

Prisoners from the upper world are tortured here, whether men, women, or children, and the awful rites performed are too fearful—so say the Indians —to be even hinted at.

The cargo first and the empty canoes next had to be portaged half a mile on shore and above the lovely linn. This was extremely hard work, but it was safely accomplished at last.

Roland was not only a born general, but a kind-hearted and excellent master. He never lost his temper, nor uttered a bad or impatient word, and thus there was not an Indian there who would not have died for him and his companion Dick.

Moreover, the officer-Indians found that kind words were more effectual than cuts with the bark whips they carried, or blows with the hand on naked shoulders.

And so the march and voyage was one of peace and comfort.

Accidents, however, were by no means rare, for there were snags and sunken rocks to be guarded against, and more than one of the small canoes were stove and sunk, with the loss of precious lives.

---

Roland determined not to overwork his crew. This might spoil everything, for many of the swamps in the neighbourhood of which they bivouacked are pestilential in the extreme.

Mosquitoes were found rather a plague at first, but our boys had come prepared.

They carried sheets of fine muslin—the ordinary mosquito-nets are useless—for if a "squeeter" gets one leg through, his body very soon wriggles after, and then he begins to sing a song of thanksgiving before piercing the skin of the sleeper with his poison-laden proboscis. But mosquitoes cannot get through the muslin, and have to sing to themselves on the other side.

After a time, however, the muslin was not thought about, for all hands had received their baptism of blood, and bites were hardly felt.

# CHAPTER XX—THE PAGAN PAYNEES WERE THIRSTING FOR BLOOD

A glance at any good map will show the reader the bearings and flow of this romantic and beautiful river, the Madeira. It will show him something else— the suggestive names of some of the cataracts or rapids that have to be negotiated by the enterprising sportsman or traveller in this wild land.

The Misericordia Rapids and the Calderano de Inferno speak for themselves. The latter signifies Hell's Cauldron, and the former speaks to us of many a terrible accident that has occurred here—boats upset, bodies washed away in the torrent, or men seized and dragged below by voracious alligators before the very eyes of despairing friends.

The Cauldron of Hell is a terrible place, and consists of a whole series of rapids each more fierce than the other. To attempt to stem currents like these would of course be madness. There is nothing for it but portage for a whole mile and more, and it can easily be guessed that this is slow and toilsome work indeed. Nor was the weather always propitious. Sometimes storms raged through the woods, with thunder, lightning, and drenching rain; or even on the brightest of days, down might sweep a whirlwind, utterly wrecking acres and acres of forest, tearing gigantic trees up by the roots, twisting them as if they were ropes, or tossing them high in air, and after cutting immense gaps through the jungle, retire, as if satisfied with the chaos and devastation worked, to the far-off mountain lands.

Once when, with their rifles in hand, Roland and Dick were watching a small flock of tapirs at a pond of water, which formed the centre of a green oasis in the dark forest, they noticed a balloon-shaped cloud in the south. It got larger and larger as it advanced towards them, its great twisted tail seeming to trail along the earth.

Lightning played incessantly around it, and as it got nearer loud peals of thunder were heard.

This startled the tapirs. They held their heads aloft and snorted with terror, running a little this way and that, but huddling together at last in a timid crowd.

Down came the awful whirlwind and dashed upon them.

Roland and Dick threw themselves on the ground, face downwards, expecting death every moment.

The din, the dust, the crashing and roaring, were terrific!

When the storm had passed not a bush or leaf of the wood in which our heroes lay had been stirred. But the glade was now a strange sight.

The waters of the pool had been taken up. The pond was dry. Only half-dead alligators lay there, writhing in agony, but every tapir had been not only killed but broken up, and mingled with twisted trees, pieces of rock, and hillocks of sand.

Truly, although Nature in these regions may very often be seen in her most beautiful aspects, fearful indeed is she when in wrath and rage she comes riding in storms and whirlwinds from off the great table-lands, bent on ravaging the country beneath.

"What a merciful escape!" said Roland, as he sat by Dick gazing on the destruction but a few yards farther off.

"I could not have believed it," returned Dick. "Fancy a whirlwind like that sweeping over our camp, Roland?"

"Yes, Dick, or over our boats on the river; but we must trust in Providence."

Roland now blew his whistle, and a party of his own Indians soon appeared, headed by a few white men.

"Boys," said Roland smiling, "my friend and I came out to shoot young tapir for you. Behold! Dame Nature has saved us the trouble, and flesh is scattered about in all directions."

The Indians soon selected the choicest, and departed, singing their strange, monotonous chant.

Presently Burly Bill himself appeared.

He stood there amazed and astonished for fully half a minute before he could speak, and when he did it was to revert to his good old-fashioned Berkshire dialect.

"My eye and Elizabeth Martin!" he exclaimed. "What be all that? Well, I never! 'Ad an 'urricane, then?"

"It looks a trifle like it, Bill; but sit you down. Got your meerschaum?"

"I've got him right enough."

And it was not long before he began to blow a kind of hurricane cloud. For when Bill smoked furnaces weren't in it.

"Do you think we have many more rapids to get past, Bill?"

"A main lot on 'em, Master Roland. But we've got to do 'em. We haven't got to funk, has we?"

"Oh no, Bill! but don't you think that we might have done better to have kept to the land altogether?"

"No," said Bill bluntly, "I do not. We never could have got along, lad. Rivers to cross by fords that we might have had to travel leagues and leagues to find, lakes to bend round, marshes and swamps, where lurks a worse foe than your respectable and gentlemanly 'gators."

"What, snakes?"

"Oh, plenty of them! But I was a-loodin' to fever, what the doctors calls malarial fever, boys.

"No, no," he added, "we'll go on now until we meet poor Benee, if he is still alive. If anything has happened to him—"

"Or if he is false," interrupted Dick; "false as Peter would have us believe—"

"Never mind wot Mr. Bloomin' Peter says! I swears by Benee, and nothing less than death can prevent his meeting us somewhere about the mouth of the Maya-tata River. You can bet your bottom dollar on that, lads."

"Well, that is the rendezvous anyhow."

"Oh," cried Dick, "sha'n't we be all rejoiced to see Benee once more!"

"God grant," said Roland, "he may bring us good news."

"He is a good man and will bring good tidings," ventured Burly Bill.

Then he went on blowing his cloud, and the boys relapsed into silence.

Each was thinking his own thoughts. But they started up at last.

"I've managed to secure a grand healthy appetite!" cried Roland.

"And so has this pale-faced boy," said Bill, shoving his great thumb as usual into the bowl of his meerschaum.

So back to camp they started.

Brawn had been on duty not far from Mr. Peter's tent, but he bounded up now with a joyful bark, and rushed forward to meet them.

He displayed as much love and joy as if he had not seen them for a whole month.

For ten days longer the expedition struggled onwards.

The work was hard enough, but it really strengthened their hearts and increased the size of their muscles, till both their calves and biceps were as hard and tough as the stays of a battle-ship.

Some people might think it strange, but it is a fact nevertheless, that the stronger they grew the happier and more hopeful were they. We may try to account for this physiologically or psychologically as we choose, but the great truth remains.

One or two of the men were struck down with ague-fever, but Roland made them rest while on shore and lie down while on board.

Meanwhile he doctored them with soup made from the choicest morsels of young tapir, with green fresh vegetable mixed therein, and for medicine they had rum and quinine, or rather, quinine in rum.

The men liked their soup, but they liked their physic better.

Between the rapids of Arara and the falls of Madeira was a beautiful sheet of water, and, being afraid of snags or submerged rocks, the canoes were kept well out into the stream.

They made great progress here. The day was unusually fine. Hot the sun was certainly, but the men wore broad straw sombreros, and, seated in the shadow of their bamboo cabin, our heroes were cool and happy enough.

The luscious acid fruits and fruit-drinks they partook of contributed largely to their comfort.

Dick started a song, a river song he had learned on his uncle's plantation, and as Burly Bill's great canoe was not far off, he got a splendid bass.

The scenery on each bank was very beautiful; rocks, and hills covered with great trees, the branches of which near to the stream with their wealth of foliage and climbing flowers, bent low to kiss the placid waters that went gliding, lapping, and purling onwards.

Who could have believed that aught of danger to our heroes and their people could lurk anywhere beneath these sun-gilt trees?

But even as they sang, fierce eyes were jealously watching them from the western bank.

Presently first one arrow, and anon a whole shower of these deadly missiles, whizzed over them.

One struck the cabin roof right above Dick's head, and another tore through the hat of the captain himself.

But rifles were carried loaded, and Roland was ready.

"Lay in your oars, men! Up, guns! Let them have a volley! Straight at yonder bush! Fire low, lads! See, yonder is a savage!"

Dick took aim at a dark-skinned native who stood well out from the wood, and fired. He was close to the stream and had been about to shoot, but Dick's rifle took away his breath, and with an agonized scream he threw up his arms and fell headlong into the water.

Volley after volley rang out now on the still air, and soon it was evident that the woods were cleared.

"Those are the Paynee Indians without a doubt," said Dick; "the same sable devils that the skipper of that steamer warned us about."

They saw no more of the enemy then, however, and the afternoon passed in peace.

An hour and a half before sunset they landed at the mouth of a small but clear river, about ten miles to the north of the Falls of Woe.

Close to the Madeira itself this lovely stream was thickly banked by forest, but the boats were taken higher up, and here excellent camping-ground was found in a country sparsely wooded.

Far away to the west rose the everlasting hills, and our heroes thought they could perceive snow in the chasms between the rocks.

Roland had not forgotten the adventure with the Indians, so scouts were sent out at once to scour the woods. They returned shortly before sunset, having seen no one.

Both Roland and Dick were somewhat uneasy in their minds, nevertheless, and after dinner, in the wan and uncertain light of a half-moon, a double row of sentries was posted, and orders were given that they should be relieved every two hours, for the night was close and sultry, just such a night as causes restless somnolence. At such times a sentry may drop to sleep leaning on his gun or against a tree. He may slumber for an hour and not be aware he has even closed an eye.

The boys themselves felt a strange drowsiness stealing away their senses. They would have rolled themselves up in their rugs and sought repose at once, but this would have made the night irksomely long.

So they chatted, and even sang, till their usual hour.

When they turned in, instead of dressing in a pyjama suit, they retained the clothes they had worn all day.

Dick noticed that Roland was doing so, and followed his example. No reason was given by his friend, but Dick could guess it. Guess also what he meant by placing a rifle close beside him and looking to his revolvers before he lay down.

Everyone in camp, except those on duty, was by this time sound asleep. Lights and fires were out, and the stillness was almost painful.

Roland would have preferred hearing the wind sighing among the forest trees, the murmur of the river, or even the mournful wailing of the great blue owl.

But never a leaf stirred, and as the moon sank lower and lower towards those strangely rugged and serrated mountains of the west, the boys themselves joined the sleepers, and all their care and anxiety was for the time being forgotten.

The night waned and waned. The sentries had been changed, and it was now nearly one o'clock.

There was a lake about a mile above the camp, that is, a mile farther westwards. It was surrounded by tall waving reeds, at least an acre wide all round.

The home *par excellence* of the dreaded 'gator was this dark and sombre sheet of water, for to it almost nightly came the tapirs to quench their thirst and to bathe.

Silently a troop of these wonderful creatures came up out of the forest to-night, all in a string, with the largest and oldest a little way in front.

Every now and then these pioneers would pause to listen. They knew the wiliness of the enemy that might be lying in wait for them. So acute in hearing are they said to be that they can distinguish the sound of a snake gliding over withered leaves at a distance of a hundred yards. But their sight also is a great protection to them. No 'gator can move among the reeds without bending them, move he never so warily. Above all this, the tapir's sense of smell is truly marvellous.

To-night the old tapirs that led the van seemed particularly suspicious and cautious. Their signal for silence was a kind of snort or cough, and this was now ofttimes repeated.

Suddenly the foremost tapir stamped his foot, and at once the whole drove turned or wheeled and glided back as silently as they had come, until the shadows of the great forest swallowed them up.

What had they seen or heard? They had seen tall, dark human figures— one, two, three—a score and over, suddenly raise their heads and shoulders above the reeds, and after standing for a moment so still that they seemed part and parcel of the solemn scene, move out from the jungle and take their way towards the slumbering camp.

Savages all, and on a mission of death.

Nobody's dreams could have been a bit more happy than those of Dick Temple just at this moment.

He was sitting once more on the deck of the great raft, which was slowly gliding down the sunlit sea-like Amazon. The near bank was tree-clad, and every branch was garlanded with flowers of rainbow hues.

But Dick looked not on the trees nor the flowers, nor the waving undulating forest itself—looked not on the sun-kissed river. His eyes were fixed on a brightly-beautiful and happy face. It was Peggy who sat beside him, Peggy to whom he was breathing words of affection and love, Peggy with shy, half-flushed face and slightly averted head.

But suddenly this scene was changed, and he awoke with a start to grasp his rifle. A shrill quavering yell rang through the camp, and awakened every echo in the forest.

The Indians—the dreaded Paynee tribe of cannibals—were on them. That yell was a war-cry. These pagan Paynees were thirsting for blood.

# CHAPTER XXI—THE FOREST IS SHEETED IN FLAMES

For just a few moments Roland was taken aback. Then, in a steady manly voice that could be heard all over the camp, he gave the order.

"All men down! The Indians are approaching from the west. Fire low, lads—between you and the light.

"Don't waste a shot!" he added.

*"FIRE LOW, LADS.... DON'T WASTE A SHOT!"*

Three Indians bit the dust at the first volley, and though the rest struggled on to the attack, it was only to be quickly repulsed.

In ten minutes' time all had fled, and the great forest and woodland was as silent as before.

It was Roland's voice that again broke the stillness.

"Rally round, boys," he shouted, "and let me know the worst."

The sacrifice of life, however, was confined to three poor fellows, one white man and two peons; and no one was wounded.

Nobody thought of going to sleep again on this sad night, and when red clouds were at last seen over the green-wooded horizon, heralding the approach of day, a general sense of relief was felt by all in the little camp.

Soon after sunrise breakfast was served, and eaten with avidity by all hands now in camp, for scouts were out, and Dick and Roland awaited the news they would bring with some degree of impatience.

The scouting was really a sort of reconnaisance in force, by picked Indians and whites under the command of the redoubtable Burly Bill.

Suddenly Brawn raised his head and gave vent to an angry "wouff!" and almost at the same time the sound of distant rifle-firing fell on the ears of the little army.

Half an hour after this, Bill and two men stepped out from the bush and advanced.

His brow was bound with a blood-stained handkerchief.

It was a spear wound, but he would not hear of it being dressed at present.

"What cheer then, Bill?"

"Not much of that," he answered, throwing himself down and lighting that marvellous meerschaum, from which he appeared to get so much consolation.

"Not a vast deal of cheer. Yes, I'll eat after I gets a bit cooler like."

"Ay, we'll have to fight the Dun-skins. They swarm in the forest between us and the Madeira, and they are about as far from bein' angels as any durned nigger could be."

"And what do you advise, Bill?"

"Well," was the reply, "as soon as your boys get their nose-bags off, my advice is to set to work with spade and shovel and transform this 'ere camp into a fortress.

"Ay, and it is one we won't be able to abandon for days and days to come," he added.

The men were now speedily told off to duty, and in a very short time had made the camp all but impregnable, and quite strong enough to give an excellent account of any number of Dun-skins.

The Paynee Indians are a semi-nomadic tribe of most implacable savages, who roam over hill and dell and upland, hunting or fighting as the case may be, but who have nevertheless a home in the dark mountain fastnesses of the far interior.

They are cannibals, though once, long, long ago, a band of Jesuits attempted their reclamation.

These brave missionaries numbered in all but one hundred and twenty men, and they went among the terrible natives with, figuratively speaking, their prayer-books in one hand, their lives in the other.

All went well for a time. They succeeded in winning the affections of the savages. They erected rude churches, and even to this day crosses of stone are to be found in this wild land, half-buried among the rank vegetation.

But there came a day, and a sad one it was, when the cannibals were attacked by a wild hill-tribe. These highlanders had heard that, owing to the new religion, their ancient enemies had degenerated into old wives and squaws.

A terrible battle ensued, during which the men from the uplands found out their mistake, for they were repulsed with fearful slaughter.

All might have gone well with the Jesuits even yet but for one contretemps.

At the very moment when the savages returned wildly exultant from the hills, bearing, horrible to relate, joints of human flesh on their spears, there came from the east a party of men who had been down to the banks of the Madeira, and had attacked and looted a small steamer that among other things had much fire-water on board.

Oh, that accursed fire-water, how terrible its results wherever on earth it gains ascendancy!

All the fearful passions of these savages were soon let loose. The scene was like pandemonium.

The poor Jesuits hid themselves in their little church, barricading the door, and devoting the first part of the night to prayer and song. But at midnight the awful howling of the cannibals coming nearer and nearer told them that they had been missed, and that their doom was now sealed.

Only one man escaped to tell the terrible tale.

And these, or rather their descendants, were the very cannibals that Roland's little army had now to do battle with.

Both he and Dick, however, kept up a good heart.

There was ammunition enough to last for months of desultory firing, if necessary, and when the attack was made at last, after Bill's scouts had been driven in, the savages learned a lesson they were never likely to forget.

Brave indeed they were, and over and over again they charged, spear in hand, almost into the trenches. But only to be thrust back wounded, or to die where they stood, beneath a steady revolver fire.

But they retreated almost as quickly as they had come, and once more sought the shelter of bush and jungle.

Not for very long, however. They were evidently determined that the little garrison should enjoy no peace.

They had changed their tactics now, and instead of making wild rushes towards the ramparts, they commenced to bombard the fort with large stones.

With their slings the Bolivian Indians can aim with great precision, for they learn the art when they are mere infants.

As no one showed above the ramparts, there was in this case no human target for the missiles, but use was made of larger stones, and these kept falling into the trenches in all directions, so that much mischief was done and many men were hurt.

A terrible rifle fire was now opened upon that part of the bush in which the cannibal savages were supposed to be in force, and from the howling and shrieking that immediately followed, it was evident that many bullets were finding their billets.

But soon even these sounds died away, and it was evident enough that the enemy had retired, no doubt with the intention of inventing some new form of attack. There was peace now for many hours, and Roland took advantage of this to order dinner to be got ready. No men, unless it be the Scotch, can fight well on empty stomachs.

The wounded were attended to and made as comfortable as possible, and after this there was apparently very little to do except to wait and watch.

Burly Bill brought out his consolatory meerschaum. But while he puffed away, he was not idle. He was thinking.

Now thinking was not very much in this honest fellow's line. Action was more his *forte*. But the present occasion demanded thought.

The afternoon was already far spent. The sentries—lynx-eyed Indians, rifles in hand—were watching the bush, and longing for a shot. Roland and Dick, with Bill and big Brawn, were seated in the shade of a green and spreading tree, and all had been silent for some considerable time.

"I say, young fellows!" said Bill at last, "this kind of lounging doesn't suit me. What say you to a council of war?"

"Well, you've been thinking, Bill?"

"Ay, I've been doin' a smart bit o' that. Let us consult Charlie."

Charlie the ex-cannibal was now brought forward and seated on the grass.

There was a deal of practical knowledge in this Indian's head. His had been a very long experience of savage warfare and wandering in forests and wilds; and he was proud now to be consulted.

"Charlie," said Bill, "what do you think of the situation?"

"De sit-uation?" was the reply. "Me not likee he. Me tinkee we sitee too much. Byme by, de cannibal he come much quick. Ah! dere will soon be muchee much too much sabage cannibal! Fust de killee you and den de eatee you, and make fine bobbery. Ha! ha!"

"Well, Charlie, I don't think that there is a deal to laugh at. Howsomever, we've got to do something soon."

"So, so," said Charlie, "notwidstanding."

"Well, I've been thinking that we should make tracks for the other side of the river. You see these savage rapscallions have no canoes, and they seem to have no food. They are not herons or storks, and can't wade through deep water."

"Foh true, sah. Dey am not stohks and dey am not herons notwidstanding, but see, sah, ebery man he am his own canoe! No stohks, but all same one frog, notwidstanding foh true!"

"And you think they would follow us?"

"All same's one eel—two hundred eel. Dey swim wid spears in mouf, and bow and arrow held high. Ha! ha! good soldier, ebery modder's son!"

"I'll tell you my plan," said Dick Temple. "Just loose off the boats, and make one bold dash for liberty."

"Ha! ha! sah!" cried Charlie. "I takes de liberty to laugh notwidstanding, foh true. You plenty much all dead men 'fore you get into de big ribber!"

"Well, hang it!" said Dick, "we're not going to stay here with the pretty prospect before us of being all scuppered and eaten. What say you, Roll?"

"I think," said Roland quietly, "that Charlie there has come prepared to speak, for his face is just beaming."

"See, sah," cried Charlie, evidently pleased, "you trust all to Charlie. He makee you free after dark. Down in de fo'est yondah dere am mebbe two, mebbee free hunder' sabages. Now dey not want to fight till de dark. Dey will fight all de same when de moon rise, and de rifle not muchee good. No hit in de dark, on'y jes' puff, puff.

"See," he continued, "de wind begin to blow a leetle. De wind get high byme by, den de sun go out, and Charlie he fiah de forest."

"Fire the forest, Charlie?"

"Notwidstanding," said Charlie grimly.

"When," he added, "you see de flame curl up, be all ready. Soon de flame he bus' highah and highah, and all by de ribber bank one big blaze."

"Charlie," cried Bill, "you're a brick! Give us a shake of your yellow hand. Hurrah! boys, Charlie's going to do it!"

Never perhaps was sunset waited for with more impatience.

The great and unanswerable question was this: Would these savages attack immediately after darkness fell, or would they take some time to deliberate?

But behind the rugged mountains down sank the sun at last, and after a brief twilight the stars shone out.

Charlie was not going alone. He had asked for the assistance of many Indians, and in a whisper he gave them their orders.

Our heroes did not interfere in any way, for fear of confusing the good fellow's plans. But they soon noted that while Charlie himself and two Indians left in one of the smallest canoes, the others disappeared like snakes in the grass, creeping northwards over the plain.

And now there was silence, for the wind was hushed; silence everywhere, that deep, indescribable silence which nightfall ever brings to a wild and savage land, in which even the beasts are still and listening in forest and dell, not knowing from which direction danger may spring.

Within the little camp nothing could be done but lie still, every man holding his breath with suspense. Nothing could be done save watch, wait, count the weary minutes, and marvel at their length.

Suddenly, however, the deep silence was broken by a mournful cry that came from riverwards. It was apparently that of an owl seeking for its mate, but it was taken up and repeated northwards all over the plain twixt camp and forest, and almost at the same time tiny tongues of fire sprang up here and there and everywhere.

Higher and higher they leapt, along the ground they ran, meeting in all directions down the dark river and across the wild moor by the edge of the woodland. The undergrowth was dry, the grass was withered, and in an amazingly short time the whole forest by the banks of the Madeira was sheeted in devastating flames.

The savages had been massed in the centre of the jungle, and just preparing to issue forth and carry death into the camp of our heroes, when suddenly the crackling of the flames fell on their ears, and they knew they were caught in a fire-trap, with scarcely any means of escape.

Charlie had been terribly in earnest, and, hurrying on in his canoe towards the Madeira, he lit the bank all along, and even down the side of the great stream itself.

It was evidently his savage intention to roast these poor cannibals alive.

As it was, the only outlet towards salvation that remained for them was the Madeira's dark brink.

"Now, boys, now!" shouted Roland, when he saw that the fire had gained entire mastery, and, making its own wind, was sweeping onwards, licking up everything in its way.

"Now, lads, on board! Let us get off down stream in all haste. Hurrah!"

# CHAPTER XXII—EVENINGS BY THE CAMP FIRE

The moorings were speedily slipped, and by the light of the blazing forest the peons bent sturdily to their paddles, and the canoe went dancing down stream.

They had already taken on board the Indians who had assisted Charlie, and before long his own boat hove in sight, and was soon taken in tow by the largest canoe.

That burning forest formed a scene which never could be forgotten. From the south side, where the boats were speedily rushing down the stream on their way to the Madeira, and from which came the light wind that was now blowing, the flames leaned over as it were, instead of ascending high in air, and the smoke and sparks took the same direction.

The sparks were as thick as snow-flakes in a snow-storm, and the lurid tongues of fire darted high as the zenith, playing with the clouds of smoke or licking them up.

The noise was indescribable, yet above the roaring and the crackling could be heard the shouts of the maddened savages, as they sought exit from the hell around them.

There was no escape except by the Madeira's bank, and to get even at this they had to dash through the burning bushes.

Alas! Charlie and his assistants had done their work all too well, and I fear that one-half of the cannibals were smothered, dragged down by alligators, or found a watery grave.

As the canoes shot past, the heat was terrible, and next morning at daybreak, when they were far up the river, towards the falls, Roland and his friend were surprised to notice that the palm-leaves which covered the cabin were brown and scorched.

On the whole the experience they had gained of the ferocity and fighting abilities of these Paynee cannibals was such as they were not likely to forget.

———————

During all this period of excitement the suspect Peter had remained perfectly quiescent. Indeed he seemed now quite apathetic, taking very little notice of anything around him, and eating the food placed before him in a way that was almost mechanical. Neither Roland nor Dick had taken much heed of him till now. When, however, they observed his strange demeanour they took council together and determined that the watch over him should be made extra strict, lest he should spring overboard and be drowned.

Roland may seem to have been harsh with Mr. Peter. But he only took proper precautions, and more than once he assured Dick that if the man's innocence were proved he would recompense him a hundred-fold.

"But," added Dick meaningly, "if he is really guilty of the terrible crime we impute to him, he cannot be punished too severely."

The expedition had that afternoon to land their stores once more to avoid rapids, and a little before sunset they encamped near to the edge of a beautiful wood well back from the banks of the Madeira.

The night passed without adventure of any kind, and everyone awoke as fresh and full of life and go as the larks that climb the sky to meet the morning sun.

Another hard day's paddling and towing and portage, and they found themselves high above the Madeira Falls in smooth water, and at the entrance to a kind of bay which formed the mouth or confluence of the two rivers, called Beni and Madro de Dios. This last is called the Maya-tata by the Bolivians.

It is a beautiful stream, overhung by hill and forest, and rises fully two hundred miles southward and west from a thousand little rivulets that drain the marvellous mountains of Karavaya.

The Beni joins this river about ten or twelve miles above the banks of the Madeira. It lies farther to the south and the east, and may be said to rise in the La Paz district itself, where it is called the Rio de la Paz.

To the north-west of both these big rivers lies the great unexplored region, the land of the Bolivian and Peruvian cannibals.

Small need have we to continue to hunt and shoot in Africa, wildly interesting though the country is, when such a marvellous tract of tens of thousands of square miles is hidden here, all unvisited as yet by a single British explorer.

And what splendid possibilities for travel and adventure are here! A land larger than Great Britain, France, and Ireland thrown together, which no one knows anything about; a land rich in forest and prairie; a land the mineral wealth of which is virtually inexhaustible; a land of beauty; a land of lake and stream, of hills and rocks and verdant prairie, and a veritable land of flowers!

A land, it is true, where wild beasts lurk and prowl, and where unknown tribes of savages wander hither and thither and hunt and fight, but all as free as the wind that wantons through their forest trees.

————————

The boats were paddled several miles up-stream to a place where the scenery was more open.

At every bend and reach of the river Roland expected to find Benee waiting for them. Perhaps he had built a hut and was living by fishing-rod and gun.

But no Benee was visible and no hut.

Together the two friends, Roland and Dick, accompanied by Charlie and Brawn, took their way across the plain and through the scrub, towards a lofty, cone-shaped hill that seemed to dominate all the scenery in its immediate neighbourhood.

To the very top of this mountain they climbed, agreed between themselves not to look back until they had reached the summit, in order that the wild beauty of this lone lorn land should burst upon them in all its glory, and at once.

They kept to their resolution, and were amply rewarded.

As far as eye could reach in any direction was a vast panorama of mountain, forest, and stream, with many a beautiful lake glittering silvery in the sunshine.

But no smoke, no indication of inhabitants anywhere.

"It seems to be quite an untenanted country we have struck," said Dick.

"All the better for us, perhaps, Dick," said Roland, "for farther we cannot proceed until poor Benee comes. He ought to have been here before now. But what adventures and dangers he may have had to pass through Heaven and himself only know."

"Charlie," he continued, "in the event of Benee not turning up within the next week or two, remember the task of guiding us to the very palace gates of the cannibal king devolves upon you."

"You speakee me too muchee fly-high Englese," said Charlie. "But Charlie he thinkee he understand. You wantee me takee you to de king's gate. I can do."

"That is enough, Charlie, and we can trust you. You have hitherto been very faithful, and what we should do without you I know not."

"Now, Dick, I guess we'll get down a little more speedily than we came up."

"We'll try, Roland, old man."

All preparations were now made to camp near to the river, where the canoes were moored.

They did not expect any attack by armed Indians, nevertheless it was deemed well to be on the safe side.

Spades and shovels were accordingly brought into use, and even before sunset a deep trench and embankment were thrown up around the tents, and at nightfall sentries were posted at each corner.

For a few days the weather was so cold and stormy that there was little comfort in either shooting or fishing. It cleared up after this, however, and at noon the sun was almost too hot.

They found caves in the rocks by the river-side in which were springs bursting and bubbling up through limestone rocks, and quartz as white as the driven snow. The water was exquisitely cool and refreshing.

The days were spent in exploring the country all around and in shooting, principally for the purpose of keeping the larder well supplied.

Luckily the Indians were very easy to please in the matter of food, though their captains liked a little more luxury.

But this land was full of game of every sort, and the river was alive with fish, and so unsophisticated were these that they sprang at a hook if it were baited only with a morsel of glittering mica picked off a rock.

What with fish and fowl and flesh of small deer, little wild pigs and the young of the tapir, there would be very little fear of starvation should they remain here for a hundred years.

Far up the Maya-tata canoe excursions were made, and at every bend of this strange river the scenery seemed more delightfully wild, silent, and beautiful.

"Heigh-ho!" said Dick one day. "I think I should not mind living here for years and years, did I but know that poor Peggy was safe and well."

"Ah! yes, that is the ever-abiding anxiety, but we are not to lose heart, are we?"

"No," said Dick emphatically. "If the worst should come to the worst, let us try to look fate fearlessly in the face, as men should."

"Bravo, Dick!"

The evenings closed in at an unconscionably early hour, as they always do in these regions, and at times the long forenights were somewhat irksome.

I have not said much about the captains of the great canoes. With one exception, these were half-castes, and spoke but little.

The exception was Don Rodrigo, who in his time had been a great traveller.

He was a man of about fifty, strongly built, but as wiry withal as an Arab of the desert.

Genial was he too, and while yarning or playing cards—the cigarette for ever in his mouth, sometimes even two—there was always a pleasant smile playing around his mouth and eyes.

He liked our young heroes, and they trusted him. Indeed, Brawn had taken to the man, and often as he squatted in the large tent of an evening, playing cards or dominoes with the boys, big Brawn would lay his honest head down on Rodrigo's knee with a sigh of satisfaction and go off to sleep.

Rodrigo could sing a good Spanish song, and had a sweet melodious voice that would have gone excellently well with a guitar accompaniment; but guitar there was none.

Versatile and clever, nevertheless, was Rodrigo, and he had manufactured a kind of musical instrument composed of pieces of glass and hard wood hung on tape bands across a board. While he sang, Rodrigo used to beat a charming accompaniment with little pith hammers.

Some of his songs were very merry indeed and very droll, and all hands used to join in the chorus, even the white men and Indians outside.

So the boys' days were for the time being somewhat of the nature of a long picnic or holiday.

The story-telling of an evening helped greatly to wile the time away.

Neither Dick nor Roland had any yarns to spin, but Charlie had stories of his wild and adventurous life in the bush, which were listened to with much pleasure. On the other hand, Rodrigo had been everywhere apparently, and done everything, so that he was the chief story-teller.

The man's English was fairly good, with just a little of the Peruvian labial accent, which really added to its attractiveness, while at times he affected the Mexican drawl.

Around the camp-fire I have seldom or never known what may be called systematic yarn-spinning. Everything comes spontaneously, one simple yarn or wild adventure leading up to the other. If now and then a song intervenes, all the better, and all the more likely is one to spend a pleasant evening either in camp or in galley on board ship.

Don Rodrigo did at times let our heroes have some tales that made their scalps creep, but they liked him best when he was giving them simple narratives of travel, and for this reason: they wanted to learn all they could about the country in which they now were.

And Rodrigo knew it well, even from Arauco on the western shore to the great marsh-lands of the Paraguay or the mountain fastnesses of Albuquerque on the east.

But the range of Rodrigo's travels was not bounded by Brazil, or the great Pacific Ocean itself. He had been a cow-boy in Mexico; he had bolo'd guanacos on the Pampas; he had wandered among the Patagonians, or on fleet horses scoured their wondrous plains; he had dwelt in the cities, or call them "towns", if so minded, that border the northern shores of the Straits of Magellan; he had even visited Tierra del Fuego—the land of fire—and from the black boats of savages had helped to spear the silken-coated otters of those wild and stormy seas; and he had sailed for years among the glorious sunlit islands of the Southern Pacific.

"As to far Bolivia," he said one evening, while his eyes followed the rings of pale-blue smoke he emitted as they rose to the tent-roof. "As to far

Bolivia, dear boys, well, you've seen a good slice of the wilder regions of it, but it is to La Paz you must some day go, and to the splendid fresh-water ocean called the Titicaca.

"Lads, I never measured it, but, roughly guessing, I should say that it is over one hundred miles in length, and in some places fifty wide."

"Wait one moment," said Burly Bill, "this is getting interesting, but my meerschaum wants to be loaded."

"Now," he added, a few minutes after, "just fire away, my friend."

# CHAPTER XXIII—A MARVELLOUS LAKE IN A MARVELLOUS LAND—LA PAZ

"Mebbe," said Rodrigo, "if you knew the down-south Bolivians as well as I do, you would not respect them a great deal. Fact is, boys, there is little to respect them for.

"Brave? Well, if you can call slaves brave, then they're about as bully's they make 'em.

"I have mentioned the inland sea called Lake Titicaca. Ah, boys, you must see this fresh-water ocean for yourselves! and if ever you get married, why, take my advice and go and spend your honeymoon there.

"Me married, did you say, Mr. Bill? It strikes me, sir, I know a trick worth several of that. Been in love as often as I've got toes and fingers, and mebbe teeth, but no tying up for life, I'm too old a starling to be tamed.

"But think, *amigo mio*, of a lake situated in a grand mountain-land, the level of its waters just thirteen thousand feet above the blue Pacific.

"Surrounded by the wildest scenery you can imagine. The wildest, ay, boys, and the most romantic.

"You have one beautiful lake or loch in your Britain—and I have travelled all over that land of the free,—I mean Loch Ness, and the surrounding mountains and glens are magnificent; but, bless my buttons, boys, you wouldn't have room in Britain for such a lake as the mighty Titicaca. It would occupy all your English Midlands, and you'd have to give the farmers a free passage to Australia."

"How do you travel on this lake?" said Dick Temple.

"Ah!" continued Rodrigo, "I can answer that; and here lies another marvel. For at this enormous height above the ocean-level, steamboats, ply up and down. No, not built there, but in sections sent from America, and I believe even from England. The labour of dragging these sections over the mountain-chains may easily be guessed.

"The steamers are neither so large nor so fine as your Clyde boats, but there is a lot of honest comfort in them after all.

"And terrible storms sometimes sweep down from the lofty Cordilleras, and then the lake is all a chaos of broken water and waves even houses high. If caught in such storms, ordinary boats are speedily sunk, and lucky are even the steamers if shelter is handy.

"Well, what would this world be, I wonder, if it were always all sunshine. We should soon get well tired of it, I guess, and want to go somewhere else—to murky England, for example."

Rodrigo blew volumes of smoke before he continued his desultory yarn.

"Do you know, boys, what I saw when in your Britain, south of the Tweed? I saw men calling themselves sportsmen chasing poor little hares with harriers, and following unfortunate stags with buck-hounds. I saw them hunt the fox too, men and women in a drove, and I called them in my own mind cowards all. Brutality and cowardice in every face, and there wasn't a farmer in the flock of stag-hunting Jockies and Jennies who could muster courage enough to face a puma or even an old baboon with a supple stick in its hand. Pah!

"But among the hills and forests around this Lake Titicaca is the paradise of the hunter who has a bit of sand and grit in his substance, and is not afraid to walk a whole mile away from a cow's tail.

"No, there are no dangerous Indians that ever I came across among the mountains and glens; but as you never know what may happen, you've got to keep your cartridges free from damp.

"What kind of game? Well, I was going to say pretty much of all sorts. We haven't got giraffes nor elephants, it is true, nor do we miss them much.

"But there are fish in the lake and beasts on the shore, and rod and gun will get but little holiday, I assure you, lads, if you elect to travel in that strange land.

"I hardly know very much about the fish. They say that the lake is bottomless, and that not only is it swarming with fish, wherever there is a bank, but that terrible animals or beasts have been seen on its deep-blue surface; creatures so fearful in aspect that even their sudden appearance has turned gray the hairs of those who beheld them.

"But I calculate that this is all Indian gammon or superstition.

"As for me, I've been always more at home in the woods and forests, and on the mountain's brow.

"I'm not going to boast, boys, but I've climbed the highest hills of the Cordilleras, where I have had no companion save the condor.

"You Europeans call the eagle the bird of Jove. If that is so, I want to ask them where the condor comes in.

"Why, your golden eagle of Scottish wilds isn't a circumstance to the condor of the Andes. He is no more to be compared to this great forest vulture than a spring chicken is to a Christmas turkey.

"But the condor is only one of a thousand wild birds of prey, or of song, found in the Andean regions or giant Cordilleras.

"And at lower altitude we find the llamas, the guanacos, and herds of wild vicuñas.

"You may come across the puma and the jaguar also, and be sorry you've met.

"Then there are goats, foxes, and wild dogs, as well as the viscacha and the chinchilla, to say nothing of deer.

"But on the great lake itself, apart from all thought of fish, you need never go without a jolly good dinner if the rarest of water-fowl will please you. Ducks and geese galore, and other species too many to name."

"That is a land, and that is a lake," said Dick musingly, "that I should dearly like to visit. Yes, and to dwell in or on for a time.

"I suppose labour is cheap?" he added enquiringly.

"I guess," returned Rodrigo, "that if you wanted to erect a wooden hut on some high and healthy promontory overlooking the lake—and this would be your best holt—you would have to learn the use of axe and adze and saw, and learn also how to drive a nail or two without doubling it over your thumb and hitting the wrong nail on the head."

"Well, anyhow," said Dick, "I shall dream to-night of your great inland ocean, of your Lake Titicaca, and in my dreams I shall imagine I am already there. I suppose the woods are alive with beautiful birds?"

"Yes," said Rodrigo, "and with splendid moths and butterflies also; so let these have a place in your dreams as well. Throw in chattering monkeys too, and beautiful parrots that love to mock every sound they hear around them. Let there be evergreen trees draped in garments of climbing flowers, roaring torrents, wild foaming rivers, that during storms roll down before them, from the flooded mountains, massive tree trunks, and boulders houses high."

"You are quite poetic!"

"But I am not done yet. People your paradise with strangely beautiful lizards that creep and crawl everywhere, looking like living flowers, and arrayed in colours that rival the tints of the rainbow. Lizards—ay, and snakes; but bless you, boys, these are very innocent, objecting to nothing except to having their tails trodden on."

"Well, no creature cares for treatment like that," said Roland. "If you and I go to this land of beauty, Dick, we must make a point of not treading on snakes' tails."

"But, boys, there are fortunes in this land of ours also. Fortunes to be had for the digging."

"Copper?"

"Yes, and gold as well!"

Rodrigo paused to roll and light another cigarette. I have never seen anyone do so more deftly. He seemed to take an acute delight in the process. He held the snow-white tissue-paper lovingly in his grasp, while with his forefinger and thumb he apportioned to it just the right quantity of yellow fragrant Virginia leaf, then twisting it tenderly, gently, he conveyed it to his lips.

Said Dick now, "I have often heard of the wondrous city of La Paz, and to me it has always seemed a sort of semi-mythical town—a South American Timbuctoo."

"Ah, lad, it is far from being mythical! On the contrary, it is very real, and so are everything and everybody in it.

"I could not, however, call it, speaking conscientiously, a gem of a place, though it might be made so. But you see, boys, there is a deal of Spanish or Portuguese blood in the veins of the real whites here—though, mind you, three-fourths of the population are Indians of almost every Bolivian race. Well, the motto of the dark-eyed whites seems to be Mañana (pronounce Mah-nyah-nah), which signifies 'to-morrow', you know. Consequently, with the very best intentions in the world, they hardly ever finish anything they begin. Some of the streets are decently paved, but every now and then you come to a slough of despond. Many of the houses are almost palatial, but they stand side by side with, and are jostled by, the vile mud-huts of the native population. They have a cathedral and a bazaar, but neither is finished yet.

"Well, La Paz stands at a great altitude above the ocean. It is well worthy of a visit. If you go there, however, there are two things you must not forget to take with you, namely, a bottle of smelling-salts and plenty of eau-de-Cologne."

"The place smells—slightly, then, I suppose," ventured Dick.

"Ha! ha! ha!" Rodrigo had a hearty laugh of his own. "Yes, it smells slightly. So do the people, I may add.

"The natives of La Paz, although some of them boast of a direct descent from the ancient Incas, are to all intents and purposes slaves.

"Well, boys, when I say 'slaves' I calculate I know pretty well what I am talking about. The old feudal system holds sway in what we call the civilized portions of Bolivia. Civilization, indeed! Only in the wilds is there true freedom and independence. The servants on ranches and farms are bought or sold with the land on which they live. So, Mr. Bill, if you purchase a farm in Bolivia, it won't be only the cows and cocks and hens you'll have to take, but the servants as well, ay, and the children of these.

"Bolivian Indians, who are troubled with families that they consider a trifle too large for their income, have a simple and easy method of meeting the difficulty. They just take what you might call the surplus children to some white-man farmer and sell them as they do their cows."

"Then these children are just brought up as slaves?"

"Yes, their masters treat them fairly well, but they generally make good use of the whip. 'Spare the rod and spoil the child' is a motto they play up to most emphatically, and certainly I have never known the rod to be spared, nor the child to be spoiled either.

"Oh! by the way, as long as my hand is in I may tell you about the servants that the gentry-folks of La Paz keep. I don't think any European would be plagued with such a dirty squad, for in a household of, say, ten, there must be ten slaves at the very least, to say nothing of the pongo man.

"This pongo man is in reality the charwoman of La Paz. It is he who does all the dirty work, and a disagreeable-looking and painfully dirty blackguard he is himself. It is not his custom to stay more than a week with any one family. He likes to be always on the move.

"He assists the cook; he collects dried llama manure for firewood, as

Paddy might say; he fetches water from the fountain; he brings home the marketing, in the shape of meat and vegetables; he cleans and scrubs everywhere, receiving few pence for his trouble, but an indefinite number of kicks and cuffs, while his bed at night is on the cold stones behind the hall door. Yet with all his ill-usage, he seems just about as happy as a New Hollander, and you always find him trotting around trilling a song.

"Ah, there is nothing like contentment in this world, boys!"

"Yes, Mr. Bill, I have seen one or two really pretty girls among the Bolivians, but never lost my heart to any of them, for between you and me, they don't either brush or comb their hair, and when walking with them it is best to keep the weather-gauge. And that's a hint worth having, I can assure you."

———————

On the very next evening after Don Rodrigo spoke his piece, as he phrased it, about the strange customs and habits of the Bolivians, all were assembled as usual in the biggest tent.

Burly Bill and his meerschaum were getting on remarkably well together, the Don was rolling a cigarette, when suddenly Brawn started up as if from a dream, and stood with his ears pricked and his head a little to one side, gazing out into the darkness.

He uttered no warning growl, and made no sound of any sort, but his tail was gently agitated, as if something pleased him.

Then with one impatient "Yap!" he sprang away, and was seen no more for a few minutes.

"What can ail the dog?" said Roland.

"What, indeed?" said Dick.

And now footsteps soft and slow were heard approaching the tent, and next minute poor Benee himself staggered in and almost fell at Roland's feet.

The honest hound seemed almost beside himself with joy, but he had sense enough to know that his old favourite, Benee, was exhausted and ill, and, looking up into his young master's face, appeared to plead for his assistance.

Benee's cheeks were hollow, his feet were cut and bleeding, and yet as he lay there he smiled feebly.

"I am happy now," he murmured, and forthwith fell asleep.

Both Roland and Dick trembled. They thought that sleep might be the sleep of death, but Don Rodrigo, after feeling Benee's pulse, assured them that it was all right, and that the poor fellow only needed rest and food.

In about half an hour the faithful fellow—ah! who could doubt his fidelity now?—sat painfully up.

Dick went hurrying off and soon returned with soup and with wine, and having swallowed a little, Benee made signs that he would rest and sleep.

"To-morrow," he said, "to-morrow I speak plenty. To-night no can do."

And so they did all they could to make him comfortable, and great Brawn lay down by his side to watch him.

# CHAPTER XXIV—BENEE'S STORY—THE YOUNG CANNIBAL QUEEN

I cannot help saying that in forbearing to talk to or to question poor Benee on the evening of his arrival, our young heroes exhibited a spirit of true manliness and courage which was greatly to their credit.

That they were burning to get news of the unfortunate Peggy goes without saying, and to hear at the same time Benee's own marvellous adventures.

Nor did they hurry the poor fellow even next day.

It is a good plan to fly from temptation, when you are not sure you may not fall. There is nothing dishonourable about such a course, be the temptation what it may.

Roland and Dick adopted the plan this morning at all events. Both were awake long before sunrise; long before the beautiful stars had ceased to glitter gem-like high over mountains and forest.

The camp was hardly yet astir, although Burly Bill was looming between the lads and the light as they stood with honest Brawn in the big tent doorway. Over his head rose a huge cloud of fragrant smoke, while ever and anon a gleam from the bowl of his meerschaum lit up his good-humoured face.

It had not taken the lads long to dress, and now they sauntered out.

The first faint light of the dawning day was already beginning to pale the stars. Soon the sun himself, red and rosy, would sail up from his bed behind the far green forest.

"Bill!"

"Hillo! Good-morning to you both! I've been up for hours."

"And we could not sleep for—thinking. But I say, Bill, I think Benee has good news. I'm burning to hear it, and so is Dick here, but it would be downright mean to wake the poor fellow till he is well rested. So, for fear we should seem too inquisitive, or too squaw-like, we're off with bold Brawn here for a walk. Yes, we are both armed."

When the lads came back in about two hours' time, they found Benee up and dressed and seated on the grass at breakfast.

When I say he was dressed I allude to the fact that he very much needed dressing, for his garments were in rags, his blanket in tatters. But he had taken the clothes Bill provided for him, and gone straight to the river for a wash and a swim.

He looked quite the old Benee on his return.

"Ah!" said Bill, "you're smiling, Benee. I know you have good news."

"Plenty good, Massa Bill, one leetle bitee bad!"

"Well, eat, old man; I'm hungry. Yes, the boys are beautiful, and they'll be here in a few minutes."

And so they were.

Brawn was before them. He darted in with a rush and a run, and licked first Benee's ears and then Bill's. It was a rough but a very kindly salute.

In these sky-high regions of Bolivia, a walk or run across the plains early in the morning makes one almost painfully hungry.

But here was a breakfast fit for a king; eggs of wild birds, fish, and flesh of deer, with cakes galore, for the Indians were splendid cooks.

Then, after breakfast, Benee told the boys and Bill all his long and strange story. It was a thrilling one, as we know already, and lost none of its effect by being related in Benee's simple, but often graphic and figurative language.

"Oh!" cried impulsive Dick, when he had finished, and there were tears in the lad's eyes that he took small pains to hide, "you have made Roland and me happy, inexpressibly happy, Benee. We know now that dear Peggy is well, and that nothing can harm her for the present, and something tells me we shall receive her safe and sound."

Benee's face got slightly clouded.

"Will it not be so, Benee?"

"The Christian God will help us, Massa Dick. Der is mooch—plenty mooch—to be done!"

"And we're the lads to do it," almost shouted Burly Bill.

"Wowff! Wowff!" barked Brawn in the most emphatic manner.

In another hour all were once more on the march towards the land of the cannibals.

---

Life at the court of Queen Leeboo, as her people called poor Peggy, was not all roses, but well the girl knew that if she was to harbour any hopes of escape she must keep cool and play her game well.

She had all a woman's wits about her, however, and all a woman's wiles. Vain Peggy certainly was not, but she knew she was beautiful, and determined to make the best use of the fact.

Luckily for her she could speak the language of this strange wild people as well as anyone, for Charlie himself had been her teacher.

A strangely musical and labial tongue it is, and figurative, too, as might be expected, for the scenery of every country has a certain effect upon its language.

It was soon evident that Queen Leeboo was expected to stay in the royal camp almost entirely.

This she determined should not be the case. So after the royal breakfast one morning—and a very delightful and natural meal it was, consisting chiefly of nuts and fruit—Queen Leeboo seized her sceptre, the poisoned spear, and stepped lightly down from her throne.

"That isn't good enough," she said, "I want a little fresh air."

Her attendants threw themselves on their faces before her, but she made them get up, and very much astonished they were to see the beautiful queen march along the great hall and step out on to the skull-decorated verandah.

The palace was built on a mountain ledge or table-land of small dimensions. It was backed by gigantic and precipitous rocks, now most beautifully draped with the greenery of bush and fern, and trailed over by a thousand charming wild flowers.

Leeboo, as we may call her for the present, seated herself languidly on a dais. She knew better than to be rash. Her object was to gain the entire confidence of her people. In this alone lay her hopes of escape, and thoughts of freedom were ever uppermost in her mind.

This was the first time she had been beyond the portals of her royal prison-house, but she determined it should not be the last.

While her attendants partially encircled her she gazed dreamily at the glorious scenery beyond and beneath her.

From her elevated position she could view the landscape for leagues and leagues on every side. Few of us, in this tame domestic land that we all love so well, have ever visited so beautiful a country as these highlands of Bolivia.

Fresh from the hands of its Maker did it seem on this fresh, cool, delightful morning. The dark green of its rolling woods and forests, the heath-clad hills, the streams that meandered through the dales like threads of silver, the glittering lakes, the plains where the llamas, and even oxen, roamed in great herds, and far, far away on the horizon the serrated mountains, patched and flecked with snow, that hid their summits in the fleecy clouds; the whole formed as grand and lovely a panorama as ever human eyes beheld.

But it was marred somewhat by the immediate surroundings of poor Leeboo.

Oh, those awful skulls! "Is everything good and beautiful in Nature," she could not help asking herself, "except mankind?"

Here was the faint odour of death, and she beheld on many of these skulls the mark of the axe, reminding her of murder. She shuddered. Her palace was but a charnel-house. Those crouching creatures around her, waiting to do her bidding or obey her slightest behest, were but slaves of tyrant masters, and every day she missed one of the youngest and fairest, and knew what her doom would be.

And out beyond the gate yonder were her soldiers, her guards. Alas, yes! and they were her keepers also.

But behold! yonder comes the great chief Kaloomah, her prime minister, and walking beside him is Kalamazoo.

Kaloomah walks erect and stately, as becomes so high a functionary. He is stern in face even to grimness and ferocity, but as handsome in form as some of the heroes of Walter Scott.

And Kalamazoo is little more than a boy, and one, too, of somewhat fragile form, with face more delicate than is becoming in a cannibal Indian.

Kalamazoo is the only son of the late queen. For some reason or other he wears a necklace of his mother's red-stained teeth. Probably they are a charm.

Both princes kneel at Leeboo's feet. Leeboo strikes both smartly on the shoulders with her sceptre and bids them stand up.

"I would not have you grovel round me," she says in their own tongue, "like two little pigs of the forest." They stand up, looking sheepish and nonplussed, and Leeboo, placing one on each side of her—a spear-length distant,—looks first at Kaloomah and then at Kalamazoo and bursts into a silvery laugh.

Why laughs Queen Leeboo? These two men are both very natural, both somewhat solemn. Not even little pigs of the forest like to be laughed at.

But the queen's mistress of the robes—let me call her so—has told her that she is expected to take unto herself a husband in three moons, and that it must be either Kaloomah or Kalamazoo.

This is now no state secret. All the queen's people know, from her own palace gates to the remotest mud hut on this cannibalistic territory. They all know it, and they look forward to that week of festivity as children in the rural districts of England look forward to a fair.

There will be a monster carousal that day.

The soldiers of the queen will make a raid on a neighbouring hill tribe, and bring back many heads and many hams.

If Kaloomah is the favourite, then Kalamazoo will be slain and cooked.

If the queen elects to smile on Kalamazoo with his necklace of the maternal molars and incisors, then Kaloomah with the best grace he can must submit to the knife.

Yet must I do justice to both and say that it is not because they fear death that they are so anxious to curry favour with the young and lovely queen. Oh no! for both are over head in love with her.

And a happy thought has occurred to Leeboo. She will play one against the other, and thus, in some way to herself at present unknown, endeavour to effect her escape from this land of murder, blood, and beautiful scenery.

So there they stand silently, a spear-length from her dais, she glorying in the power she knows she has over both. There they stand in silence, for court etiquette forbids them to speak until spoken to.

Very like a couple of champion idiots they are too. Big Kaloomah doesn't quite know what to do with his hands, and Kalamazoo is fidgeting nervously with his necklace, and apparently counting his dead mother's teeth as monks count their beads.

Leeboo rises at last, and, gathering the loose portion of her skirts around her, says: "Come, I would walk."

She is a little way ahead, and she waves her spear so prettily as she smiles her sweetest and points to the grimly ornamental gate.

And after hesitating for one moment, both Kaloomah and the young prince follow sheepishly.

The guards by the gate, grim, fully armed cut-throats, seeing that her majesty expects obedience, fall back, and the trio march through.

But I do not think that either of Leeboo's lovers is prepared for what follows.

If they had calculated on a solemn majestic walk around the plateau, they were soon very much undeceived.

Leeboo had no sooner begun to breathe the glorious mountain air, than she felt as exuberant as a child again. Indeed, she was but little else. But she placed her spear and sceptre of royalty very unceremoniously into Kaloomah's hand to hold, while she darted off after a splendid crimson specimen of dragon-fly.

Kaloomah looked at Kalamazoo. Kalamazoo looked at Kaloomah.

The one didn't love the other, it is true, yet a fellow-feeling made them wondrous kind. And the feeling uppermost in the mind of each was wonder.

Kaloomah beckoned to Kalamazoo, and pointed to the queen. The words he spoke were somewhat as follows:

"Too much choorka-choorka! Suppose the queen we lose—"

He pointed with his thumb to his neck by way of completing the sentence.

"Too much choorka-choorka!" repeated the young prince. "You old— you stop her."

"No, no, you young—you run quick, you stop her!"

That dragon-fly gave Leeboo grand sport for over half an hour. From bush to bush it flitted, and flew from flower to flower, over rocks, over cairns, and finally down the great hill that led to the plain below.

Matters looked serious, so both lovers were now in duty bound to follow their all-too-lively queen.

When they reached the bottom of the brae, however, behold!—but stay, there was no behold about it. Queen Leeboo was nowhere to be seen!

# CHAPTER XXV—BENEE'S MOTHER TO THE FRONT

Here was a difficulty!

If they returned without the queen, they would be torn in pieces and quietly eaten afterwards.

They became excited. They looked here, there, and everywhere for Leeboo. Up into the trees, under the bushes, behind rocks and stones, but all in vain. The beautiful girl seemed to have been spirited away, or the earth had opened and admitted her into fairy-land, or—

But see! To their great joy, yonder comes the young queen holding aloft the dragon-fly and singing to herself.

Not a whit worse was the lovely thing; not one of its four gauzy wings was so much as rumpled.

Then she whispered something to it, and tossed it high in air.

And away it flew, straight to the north-east, as if bent upon delivering the message she had entrusted to its keeping.

She stood gazing after it with flushed cheeks and parted lips until it was no longer visible against the sky's pale blue, then turned away with a sigh.

But Leeboo was not tired yet. There were beautiful birds to be seen and their songs listened to. And there were garlands of wild flowers to be strung.

One she threw over Kaloomah's neck.

Kalamazoo looked wretched.

She made him even a larger, and he was happy. This garland quite hid his mother's frightful teeth.

But it must be said that these two lovers of Leeboo's looked—with those garlands of flowers around their necks—more foolish than ever.

She trotted them round for two whole hours. Then she resumed her sceptre, and intimated her intention to return to the palace.

For a whole week these rambles were continued day after day.

Then storm-winds blew wild from off the snow-patched mountains, and Leeboo was confined to her palace for days.

Her maids of honour, however, did all they could to please and comfort her. They brought her the choicest of fruits, and they told her strange weird tales of strange weird people and mannikins who in these regions dwell deep down in caves below the ground, and often steal little children to nurse their tiny infants.

And they sang or chanted to her also, and all night long in the drapery-hung chamber, where she reposed on a couch of skins, they lay near her, ready to start to their feet and obey her slightest command.

Leeboo ruled her empire by love. But she could be haughty and stern when she pleased, only she never made use of that terrible spear, one touch of which meant death.

--------

In less than six-weeks' time Queen Leeboo had so thoroughly gained the confidence of her people that she was trusted to go anywhere, although always under the eyes of the young prince or Kaloomah.

I believe Leeboo would have learned to like the savages but for their cannibal tastes, and several times, when men returned from the war-path, she had to witness the most terrible of orgies.

It was always young girls or boys who were the victims of those fearful feasts. Her heart bled for them, but all remonstrance on her part was in vain.

Leeboo had got her pony back, and often had a glorious gallop over the prairie.

But something else had happened, which added greatly to Leeboo's comfort and happiness. Shooks-gee himself came to camp and brought with him little Weenah, his beautiful child-daughter.

Leeboo took to her at once, and the two became constant companions.

Weenah could converse in broken English, and so many a long delightful "confab" they had together.

Child-like, Weenah told Leeboo of her love for Benee, of their early rambles in the forest, too, and of her own wild wanderings in search of him. Told her, too, that Benee was coming back again with a fresh army of Indians and white men, with Leeboo's own lover and her brother as their captains; told her of the fearful fight that was bound to take place, but which would end in the complete triumph of the good men and the rescue of Leeboo herself.

Yes, Weenah had her prophecy all cut and dry, and her story ended with a good "curtain", as all good stories should.

Whether Weenah's prophecy would be fulfilled or not we have to read on to see, for, alas! it was a dark and gloomy race of savages that would have to be dealt with, and rather than lose their queen, Kaloomah and his people would—but there! I have no wish to paint my chapters red.

———

Leeboo was not slow to perceive that her chief chance of escape lay in the skill with which she might play her two lovers against each other.

Whoever married her would be king. He would rank with, but after, the queen herself, for, to the credit of these cannibals be it said, they always prefer female government.

In civilized society Leeboo might have been accused of acting mischievously; for she would take first one into favour and then the other, giving, that is, each of them a taste of the seventh heaven time about. When Kalamazoo's star was in the ascendant, then Kaloomah was deep down in a pit of despair; but anon, he would be up and out again, and then it was

Kalamazoo's turn to weep and wail and gnash his triangular red-stained teeth.

It is needless to say that the game she was playing was a sad strain upon our poor young heroine. No wonder her eyes grew bright with that brightness which denotes loss of strength, and weariness, and that her cheeks were often far too flushed.

Hope deferred makes the heart sick, and but for little Weenah I think that Leeboo would have given up heart altogether and lain down to die.

But Weenah was always bright, cheerful, and happy. She was laughing all day long. Benee was coming for her; of that she was very certain and sure, so she sang about her absent lover even as birds in the woodlands sing, and with just as sweet a voice.

The plot was thickening and thickening, and Leeboo managed matters now so that only one of her guardians at a time accompanied herself and Weenah in their rides or rambles.

Dixie—as the pony was named—was a very faithful little horse, and though when Weenah had to trot beside him he never was allowed to go the pace, he was exceedingly strong, and could scour the plain or prairie as fleet as the wind whenever his young mistress put him on his mettle. On such occasions, no matter which of Leeboo's admirers was with her, he dropped far astern, and after running for a mile or so, had to sit down to pant.

But the young queen always returned, and so she was trusted implicitly.

So too was Weenah, but then Weenah was one of themselves.

————

In their very long and toilsome march, up the Mayatata, well was it indeed for Roland and Dick that they had guides so faithful and clever as Benee and Charlie. But for them, indeed, the expedition would have been foredoomed to failure.

Benee indeed was really the guiding star. For in his own lonesome wanderings he had surveyed the whole country as it were, and knew every fitting place for a camp, every ford on every stream, and every pathway through the dense and dark forests.

They were but the pathways made by the beasts, however, and often all but impassable. Still, in single file they marched, and were always successful in making their way. Two whole months passed away, and now, as they were nearing the cannibal highlands, greater precautions than ever were required.

And for a week they had to turn night into day, and travel while the savages slept.

They kept away, too, from any portion of the country which seemed to have the slightest claim to be called inhabited. Better they should herd with the wild beasts of the forest than sight the face of even a single savage. For swift as deer that savage would run towards the cannibal head-quarters and give information of the approach of a pale-face horde of enemies.

At last there came a day when Benee called a council of war.

"We now get near de bad man's land," he said. "Ugh! I not lub mooch blood."

"Then what would you have us do?" said Roland. "Shall we advance boldly or make a night attack?"

"No, no, no, sah. Too many cannibal warrior, too much pizen arrow, sling, and spear. No; build here a camp. Make he strong. Benee will go all same. Benee will creep and crawl till he come to father and mother house. Den Benee make all right. Pray for Benee."

Benee left, poor Brawn bidding him a most affectionate farewell. Surely that honest dog knew he was bent on saving his little mistress, if only he could.

Charlie, the ex-cannibal, stayed in camp for the time being, but he might be useful as a spy afterwards.

It is needless to say that the prayers of both our heroes were offered up night and day for Benee's success, and that their blessings followed him.

But we do not always receive the answers that would appear to us the best to our prayers, however earnest and heartfelt they may be. Still, we know well, though we are generally very loth to admit it, that afflictions are very often blessings in disguise.

And now Benee was once more all alone on the war-path, and he followed his old tactics, creeping quietly through the jungle only by night, and retiring into hiding whenever day began to obliterate the stars. Roland gave orders for the camp to be immediately fortified. It was certainly a well-chosen one, on the top of a wooded hill.

This hill was scarcely a hundred feet high, but although it might be taken by siege, its position rendered it almost impregnable as far as assault was concerned.

A rampart with a trench was thrown round three sides of it. That was apparently all that would be needed.

Looking from below by daylight even, hardly a savage could have told that an enemy held the hill.

And now there was nothing to do but to wait. And waiting is always wearisome work.

But let us follow Benee.

His progress was slow, but it was sure, and at last he reached the cottage where good Shooks-gee and his wife resided.

But here was no one save his "mother", as Benee lovingly called her.

A great fear took possession of his mind. Could it be that his father himself was dead, and that Weenah was captive?

His lips and voice almost refused to formulate the question nearest to his heart.

But his mother's smile reassured him. Weenah was safe, and at the court of the queen, and Shooks-gee himself was there. So Benee grew hopeful once more.

But his task would be by no means an easy one.

First and foremost he must establish communication between the captive girl and himself. How could this be done?

Had Shooks-gee been at home it might have been managed simply enough. But he himself dared not appear anywhere in sight of the savages.

He felt almost baffled, but at last his mother came to his rescue.

The risk would be extreme. These cannibal savages are as suspicious of strangers as they are fierce and bloodthirsty, and if this poor, kindly-hearted woman was taken for a spy her doom would be sealed.

But see the young queen she must, or little Weenah, her daughter; for great though Benee's abilities were, he did not possess the accomplishment of writing.

----------

Dressed as one of the lowest of peasants, the mother of Weenah set boldly out on her forlorn hope the very next day, and in the afternoon she was within one mile of the palace itself.

Here she hid herself in the jungle, and after eating a little fruit went to sleep.

The stars were still shining when she awoke, but she knew them all, and those that were setting told her that day would soon break.

To pass through the soldier-guards and enter the palace would, she knew, be an utter impossibility. There was nothing for it but to wait with patience, for her husband had told her that the queen rode out for a scamper over the plains every forenoon.

He had even told her the direction she usually took, not riding fast, but with Weenah running by her side, keeping a long way ahead of her lover guardian, whichever one of them might happen for the time being to be the happy man.

Benee's mother was as courageous as a mountain cat. She had a duty to perform, and she meant to carry it out.

Well, we are told in some old classic that fortune favours the brave.

It does not always do so, but in this case, at all events, this good woman was successful.

At a certain part of the plain there were bushes close and thick enough, and just here Leeboo with her little charger must pass if she came out to-day at all.

It was at this spot, then, that Weenah's mother concealed herself.

Nor had she very long to wait, for soon the sound of the pony's hoofs fell on her ear, beating a pleasant accompaniment to two sweet voices raised in song.

The Indian woman raised herself and peeped over the bushes.

Yes, they were coming, and alone too, for Kaloomah could not run so fast as Kalamazoo, and was a long way behind.

With characteristic impulse Weenah rushed forward and was clasped for a moment in her mother's arms.

And, somewhat astonished, Leeboo immediately reined up.

# CHAPTER XXVI—THE PALE-FACE QUEEN HAS FLED

Leeboo, the young queen, could see that the woman was flurried and excited.

She stood with her face to the pony and one arm was held aloft in the air. Her eyes were gleaming, and her hat had fallen over her back, allowing her wealth of coal-black hair to escape.

Weenah stood by the saddle.

"I have that to say," exclaimed her mother, in her strangely musical language, "that must be said speedily. If I am seen we are all doomed. But listen, and listen intently. You are free if you are fortunate. Liberty is at hand. Your friends are twenty miles down stream in camp. Down the stream of Bitter Waters. Ride this way to-morrow, and when far enough away take Weenah in your saddle, and gallop for your life into the forest. Weenah will be your guide."

So quickly did the woman vanish that for a few moments our heroine half believed she must have been dreaming.

But she pulled herself together at once, and now rode back to meet Kaloomah.

She was all smiles too.

"Why waits poor Kaloomah here?" she said, in her softest sweetest tones.

Kaloomah placed his hand on the saddle pommel, and panted somewhat. But Kaloomah was in the seventh heaven.

"Say—say—say 'poor Kaloomah' again," he muttered.

"Poor Kaloomah! Poor dear Kaloomah!"

She could even afford to place emphasis on the "dear", she was so happy.

"Oh—ugh!" sighed the savage; "but to-morrow it may be 'poor dear Kalamazoo!'"

"Ah, you are jealous! A little forest bird is pecking, pecking at your heart. But listen; to-morrow it shall not be Kalamazoo, but Kaloomah once again."

Well, I dare say that love-making is very much the same all over the wide, wide world, and so we cannot even laugh at this cannibal if he did bend rapturously down and kiss the toe of Leeboo's sandal-shaped stirrup.

"And now, Kaloomah," she added, "I would gather some wild flowers, and listen for a little while to the soo-soo's song while you twine my wild flowers into a garland. My little handmaiden, Weenah, will assist you.

"But, Kaloomah!" she continued archly.

"Yes, my moon-dream."

"You must not make love to my maiden, else a little forest bird will peck poor Leeboo's heart to pieces and Leeboo die."

———

I hardly think it would be putting it one whit too strongly to say that the pale-face maiden queen had turned this savage's head.

They all returned together at last to the palace, and the queen with her little handmaiden retired to her chamber to dine.

As to Kaloomah, the spirit of pride had got into him, and this is really as difficult to get rid of as if one were possessed of an evil spirit. So the chief, decorated with the garland of wild flowers that Leeboo the queen had placed around his neck, could not resist the temptation to parade himself on the plateau before Kalamazoo's tent. He wished the prince to see him. And the prince did.

The prince, moreover, was strongly tempted to rush forth, spear in hand, and slay his rival where he stood.

But he remembered in time that Kaloomah was not only a great chief but a mighty warrior. Over and over again had he led the cannibal army against the glens and valleys of distant highland chiefs. And he had been ever victorious, his soldiers returning after a great slaughter of the foe, laden with heads and hams, to hold nights and nights of fearful orgie.

Kalamazoo knew that Kaloomah was the people's favourite, and that if he slew him, he himself would speedily be torn limb from limb.

So he was content to gnash his own teeth, to count his mother's over and over again, and to remain quiescent.

It is seldom indeed that a savage is troubled with sleeplessness, but that night poor Benee was far too anxious to slumber soundly. For he knew not what another day might bring forth. It might be pregnant with happiness for him and the young girls he loved so dearly, or it might end in bloodshed and in death.

What a glorious morning broke over the woodlands at last! Looking eastwards Benee could note a strip of the deepest orange just above the dark forest horizon. This faded into palest green, and above all was ethereal blue, with just one or two rosy clouds. And westwards those patches of snow in the hollow of the mighty Sierras were pink, with purple shadows.

And this innocent and unsophisticated savage bent himself low on his knees and prayed to Him who is the author of all that is beautiful, to bless his enterprise and take his little mistress safe away from this blood-stained land of darkness and woe.

He felt better when he rose to his feet. Then he entered the cottage and had breakfast.

"I will come again some day," he said, as his "mother" bade him a tearful farewell. "I will come again and take Father and you to the far-off happy land of the pale-faces."

So he hied him away to the forest, looking back just once to wave his hand.

He well knew the road that Weenah and Leeboo—no, let us call her Peggy once more—would take, if indeed they should succeed in escaping.

He walked towards the river of Bitter Waters therefore, and, journeying for some miles along its wild romantic banks, lay down to wait.

Wild flowers trailed and climbed among the bushes where he hid; he saw not their bright colours, he was scarcely sensible of their perfume.

The soo-soo's song was sweet and plaintive; he heard it not.

He was wholly absorbed in thought. So the sun got higher and higher, and still he waited and watched—waited and hoped.

Only, ever and anon he would place his ear against the hard ground and listen intently.

'Twas noon, and they came not.

Something must have happened. Everything must have failed.

What should he do? What could he do?

---

But hark! A joyful sound. It was that of a horse at the gallop, and it was coming nearer and nearer.

Benee grasped his rifle.

It must be she. It must, and was poor Peggy, and Weenah was seated behind her.

He looked quickly to his repeating rifle, and patted the revolvers in his belt.

"Oh, Benee, Benee! how rejoiced I am!"

"But are you followed, Missie Peggy?"

"No, no, Benee, we have ridden clean and clear away from the savage chief Kaloomah, and we fear no pursuit."

"Ah, Missie! You not know de savage man. I do. Come. Make track now.

"Weenah," he added. "Oh, my love, Weenah! But come not down. We mus' fly foh de cannibal come in force."

It seemed but child's play to Benee to trot lightly along beside the pony.

Love, no doubt, made the labour lighter. Besides, on faithful little Dixie's back was all that Benee cared much for in the world, Weenah and "Missie Peggy".

True enough, he liked and respected Roland, and Dick as well, but they were not all the world to him as these girls were. And ever since he had found Roland and Peggy in the dark forest and rescued them, his little mistress had been in his eyes an angel. Never an unkind word was it possible for her to say to anyone, least of all—so he flattered himself—to Benee.

The poor, untutored savage felt, in his happiness, at this moment, that it would be sweet to die were the loved ones only near to hold his hand.

But he could die, too, fighting for them; ay, fighting to the end. Who was he that would dare touch the ground where Peggy or Weenah trod if he— Benee—were there?

And so they journeyed on and on by the river's side and through jungle and forest, never dreaming of danger or pursuit.

Ah! but wild as a panther was Kaloomah now.

When he found that he was baffled, befooled, deserted, then all his fury —the fury of an untamed savage—boiled up from the bottom of his heart.

Love! Where was love now? It found no place in this wild chief's heart; hate had supplanted it, and it was a hate that must be quenched in blood. Yes, her blood! He would be revenged, and then—well then, the sooner he should die after that the better. For his life's sun had gone out, his days could only be days of darkness now.

Yet how happy had he been only this morning, and how proud when he stalked forth from his hut and passed that of Kalamazoo, still wearing the wild flowers with which she had adorned him!

He tore those wild flowers from his neck now, and scattered them to the winds.

Then, as fast and fleet as ever savage ran, he hied him back to the palace.

Few had more stentorian lungs than Kaloomah!

"The queen has gone! The white queen has fled!"

That shout awakened one thousand armed men to action, and in less than an hour they were on the warpath.

# CHAPTER XXVII—THE FIGHT AT THE FORT

So toilsome was the road to trace, and so far away was the fortified camp of our heroes, that the sun was almost setting before Benee arrived with his precious charge.

Why should I make any attempt to describe the meeting of Roland and Dick with the long-lost Peggy?

Roland and she had always been as brother and sister, and now that they were once more united, all her joy found vent in a flood of tears, which her brother did what he could to stem.

It seemed hardly possible that she should be here safe and sound, and in the presence of those who loved her so well and dearly.

And here, too, was Brawn, who was delirious with joy, and honest Bill with his meerschaum.

"Oh, surely I shall not awake and find it all a dream!" she cried in terror. "Awake and find myself still in that awful palace, with its dreadful surroundings and the odour of death everywhere! Oh—h!"

The girl shuddered.

"Dear Peggy," said Dick tenderly, "this is no dream; you are with us again, and we with you. All the past is as nothing. Let us live for the future. Is that right, Roland?"

"Yes, you must forget the past, Peggy," said Roland. "Dick is right. The past shall be buried. We are young yet. The world is all before us. So come, laugh, and be happy, Peggy."

"And this charming child here, who is she?" said Dick. He alluded to Weenah.

"That is little Weenah, a daughter of the wilds, a child of the desert. Nay, but no child after all, are you, Weenah?"

Weenah bent her dark eyes on the ground.

"I am nothing," she said. "I am nobody, only—Benee's."

"But, Weenah," said Peggy, taking the girl by the hand, "oh, how I shall miss you when you go!"

"Go?" said Weenah wonderingly.

"Yes, dear, you have a father and a mother, who are fond of you. Must you not return soon to them?"

"My father and my mother I love," replied Weenah. "And you I love, for you have taught me to pray to the pale-face's God. You have taught me many, many things that are good and beautiful. My life now is all joy and brightness, and so, though I love my mother and my father, oh! bid me not to leave you."

All this was spoken in the language of the country. It was Greek to those around them, but even Bill could see that the dark-eyed maiden was pleading for something, for her hand was in Peggy's, her eyes upon hers.

---

It was just at this moment that scouts came hurrying in from the forest, bringing news that was startling enough, as well as surprising.

These men had come speedily in, almost as fleet of foot as deer, and the word they brought was that the savages, at least six hundred strong, were not more than three hours distant.

Roland showed no excitement, whatever he might feel. Nor did Dick. Yet both were ready for action.

Burly Bill, who had been quietly smoking a little way off, put his great thumb in the bowl of his meerschaum, and stowed away that faithful companion of his in his coat-pocket.

Can a young fellow still in his teens, and whom we older men are all too apt to sneer at as a mere boy, prove himself a good general. He may and he can, if he has grit in him and a head of some sort surmounting his shoulders.

From what followed I think Roland proved that he was in possession of both.

Well, he had descended from a long line of hardy Cornish ancestors, and there is more in good blood than we are apt to believe.

He came to the front now at all events, and Dick and Bill, to say nothing of Benee, Rodrigo, and the other canoe captains, were ready to obey his every command.

Roland called a council of war at once, and it did not take long to come to a decision.

Our chief hero was the principal speaker. But brave men do not lose much time in words.

"Boys," he said, "we've got to fight these rascally savages. That's so, I think?"

"That's so," was the chorus.

"Well, and we've got to beat them, too. We want to give them something that shall keep them both quiet and civil until we can afford to send out a few missionaries to improve their morals.

"Now, Rodrigo, I cannot force you to fight."

"Force, sir? I need no force. Command me."

"Well, I will. I wish to outflank these beggars. You and our Indians, with Benee as your guide, are just the men to do so.

"The moon will be up in another hour. It will be the harvest-moon in England. The harvest-moon here, too—but a harvest, alas! of blood.

"Now, Benee," he continued, "as soon as we are ready, guide these men with Captain Rodrigo for some distance down-stream, then curl round the savages, and when they begin to retreat, or even before that, attack them in the rear. Good luck to you!"

As silently as ghosts two hundred and fifty well-armed Indians, a short time after Roland made that brave little speech, glided down the brow of the hill, and disappeared in the woods beyond.

Though our heroes listened, they could not hear a sound, not even the crackling of a bush or broken branch.

Soon the moon glared red through the topmost boughs of the far-off trees, and flooded all the land with a light almost as bright as day. The stars above, that before had glittered on the river's rippling breast, and the stars beneath—those wondrous flitting fire-insects—paled before its beams, and the night-birds sought for shelter in caves among the rocks. So over all the prairie and woodlands there fell a stillness that was almost oppressive. It was as if Nature held her breath, expectant of the fight that was to follow.

Nor was that fight very long delayed. But it must have been well on towards midnight before the first indication of an approaching foe was made manifest.

Only a long, mournful hoot, away in the bush, and bearing a close resemblance to that of the owl.

It was repeated here and there from different quarters, and our heroes knew that an attack was imminent.

There was in the centre of the camp a roomy cave. In this all stores had been placed, with water enough for a night at all events, and here were Peggy and Weenah safely guarded by Brawn. Roland had managed to make the darkness visible by lighting two candles and placing them on the wall.

In a smaller cave was Peter, and as he had given evidence lately of a great desire to escape, the boys had taken the liberty to rope him.

"You shall live to repent this," hissed the man through his teeth.

He had thrown overboard all his plausibility now, and assumed his natural self—the dangerous villain.

"Have a care," replied Dick, "or you will not live long enough to repent of anything."

On one side of the camp was the river, down under a cliff of considerable height. It was very quiet and sluggish just here, and its gentle whispering was no louder than a light breeze sighing through forest trees.

There were, therefore, really only three sides of the parapet and hill to defend.

And now Burly Bill's quick ear caught the sound of rustling down below.

"The savages are on us," he said quietly.

"Then give them a volley to begin with," answered Roland.

The white men started down scores of huge stones; but this was more for the purpose of bringing the savages into sight than with a view to wound or kill any.

It had the desired effect, and probably another, for the cannibals must have believed the pale-faces had no other means of defence.

They were seen now in the bright moonlight scrambling up-hill in scores, with knives in their mouths and spears on their backs.

"Fire straight and steadily, men," cried the young chief, Roland. "Fire independently, and every man at the enemy in front of him."

A well-aimed and rattling volley, followed by another and another, made the Indians pause. The number of dead and wounded was great, and impeded the progress of those who would have rushed up and on.

Volley after volley was now poured into the savage ranks, but they came pressing up from behind as black and fierce and numerous as a colony of mountain-ants.

Their yelling and war-cries were terrible to hear.

But the continuous volley-firing still kept them at bay.

"The rockets, Dick, are they ready?"

"Yes, captain, all ready."

"Try the effect of these."

It was a fearful sight to witness those dread weapons of warfare tear through the ranks of these shrieking demons.

Death and mutilation was dealt on every side, and the fire from the ramparts grew fiercer and fiercer.

Yet so terrible in their battle-wrath are these cannibals, that—well our heroes knew—if they were to scale the ramparts, even the white men would not be able to stand against them.

Then the fight would degenerate into a massacre, and this would be followed by an orgie too awful to contemplate.

At this moment there could not have been fewer than five hundred savages striving to capture the little hill on which stood the camp, and Roland's men in all were barely eighty. Some who had exposed themselves were speedily brought down with poisoned arrows, and already lay writhing in the agonies of spasmodic death.

But see, led on by the chief Kaloomah himself, who seems to bear a charmed life, the foremost ranks of those sable warriors have already all but gained footing on the ramparts, while with axe and adze the pale-faces endeavour to repel them.

In vain!

Kaloomah—great knife in hand—and at least a score of his braves have effected an entrance, and the whites, though fighting bravely, are being pushed, if not driven back.

It is a terrible moment!

# CHAPTER XXVIII—THE DREAM AND THE TERROR!

Far more acute in hearing are these children of the wilds than any white man who ever lived, and now, just as hope was beginning to die out of even Roland's heart, a sudden movement on the part of the savages who had gained admittance caused him to marvel.

More quickly than they had entered, back they sprang towards the parapet, and on gazing after them, our heroes found that the hill-sides were clear.

It was evident, however, that a great battle was going on down beneath on the prairie.

Explanation is hardly needed.

Rodrigo's men, guided by Benee, had outflanked—nay, even surrounded—the foe, and with well-aimed volleys had thrust them back and back towards the river, into which, with wild agonizing shouts, all that was left of Kaloomah's army was driven.

They were excellent swimmers, the 'gators were absent from this river, and doubtless hundreds of fugitives would find their way back into their own dark land to tell how well and bravely the pale-faces can fight.

But Kaloomah, where is he?

Intent on revenge, even while the battle raged the fiercest and the whites were being driven back, his quick eye caught the glimmer of the candle-light in the cave.

Leeboo was there, he told himself, and the false witch Weenah.

He shortened his knife, and made a rush for the entrance.

"Hab—a—rabb—rr—rr—ow!" That was the voice of the great wolf-hound, as he sprang on the would-be assassin and pinned him to the ground.

Kaloomah's knife dropped from his hand as he tried to free himself.

But Brawn had him by the throat now, and had not brave Peggy sprung to the assistance of the savage, the dog would have torn the windpipe from his neck.

But Kaloomah was prisoner, and when the fight was all over, the dog was released from duty, and the chief was bound hand and foot and placed in the other cave beside Peter.

This cave, which had thus been turned into a prison, possessed an entrance at the side, a kind of doorway through the dark rocks, and a great hole at the top, through which daylight, or even moonlight, could stream. At some not very distant date it had evidently been used as a hut, and must have been the scene of many a fearful cannibal orgie, for scores of human skulls were heaped up in corners, and calcined bones were also found. Altogether, therefore, an unhallowed kind of place, and eerie beyond conception.

It is as well to tell the truth concerning the battle on the hill-top, ghastly though it may appear. There were no wounded men there, for even in the thick of the fight the savages not only slew the white men who dropped, but their own maimed as well.

So long as the brave fellows under Roland and Dick held the ramparts, and poured their volleys into the ranks of the enemy beneath, scarcely a white man was hurt; but when the battlements were carried by storm, then the havoc of war commenced in earnest; and at daylight a great deep trench was excavated, and in this no fewer than eleven white men were placed, side by side.

A simple prayer was said, then a hymn was sung—a sad dirge-like hymn to that sacred air called "Martyrdom", which has risen in olden times from many a Scottish battle-field, where the heather was dripping blood. I take my fiddle and play it now, and that mournful scene rises up before me, in which the white men crowd around the long quiet grave, where their late companions lie sleeping in the tomb.

Every head is bared in the morning sunshine, every eye is wet with tears.

It is Bill himself who leads the melody.

Then clods are gently thrown upon the dead, and soon the grave is filled.

———————

There was not the slightest apprehension now that the battle would be renewed, and so all the day was spent in getting ready for the long march back to the spot where, under the charge of one of the captains and his faithful peons, the great canoes had been left.

Among the stores brought here to camp—the suggestion had emanated from Roland's mother and Beeboo—was a chest containing many changes of raiment and dresses belonging to Peggy. In the cave, then, both she and Weenah conducted their toilet, and when, some time after, and just as breakfast was about to be served, they both came out, it would have been difficult, indeed, to keep from exclamations of surprise.

Even Benee gave way to his excitement, and, seizing Weenah, held her for a moment high in air.

"I rejoice foh true!" he cried. "All ober my heart go flapperty-flap. Oh, Weenah! you am now all same one red pale-face lady."

Dick thought Peggy, with her bonnie sun-tanned face, more lovely now than ever he had seen her.

———————

But while they are breakfasting, and while the men are quietly but busily engaged getting the stores down-hill, let us take a peep into the cave where the prisoners are.

When Kaloomah was thrust into the cave, Peter was fast asleep. Of late he had become utterly tired and careless of life. Was his not a wrecked existence from beginning to end? This was a question that he oftentimes asked himself sadly enough.

During the fight that had raged so long and fiercely he had remained perfectly passive. What was it to him who won or who lost? If the Indians won, he would speedily be put out of pain. If the white men were the victors —well, he would probably die just the same. At all events, life was not worth having now.

Then, when the lull of battle came, when the wild shrieks and shouting were over, and when the rattling of musketry was no longer heard, he felt utterly tired. He would sleep, he told himself, and what cared he if it should be

> "The sleep that knows not breaking,
>
> Morn of toil or night of waking"?

The cords that bound him hurt a little, but he would not feel their pressure when—he slept.

His was not a dreamless sleep by any means, though a long one.

His old, old life seemed to rise up before him. He was back again in England—dear old England! He was a clerk, a confidential clerk.

He had no care, no complications, and he was happy. Happy in the love of a sweet girl who adored him; the girl that he would have made his wife. Poor? Yes, both were; but oh! when one has innocence and sweet contentment, love can bloom in a garret.

Yet envy of the rich began to fill his soul. The world was badly divided. Why had he to tread the streets day after day with muddy boots to his office, and back to his dingy home after long hours of toil and drudgery at the desk?

Oh for comfort! Oh for riches!

The girl that was to be his was more beautiful than many who lolled in cushioned carriages, with liveried servants to attend their beck and call.

So his dream went on, and dreams are but half-waking thoughts.

But it changes now!

He sees Mary his sweetheart, wan and pale, with tears in her eyes for him whose voice she may never hear again.

For the tempter has come with gold and with golden promises.

And he has fallen!

Other men have fallen before. Why not he when so much was to be gained? So much of—nay, not of glory, but of gold. What is it that gold cannot do?

A conscience? Yes, he had possessed one once. But this tempter had laughed heartily when he talked of so old-fashioned a possession. It was all a matter of business.

Behold those wealthy men who glide past in their beautiful landaus. Did they have consciences? If they did, then, instead of a town and country house, their home would soon be the garret vile in some back slum in London.

Again the dream changes. To the fearful and awful now. For, stretched out before him is Mary, wan and worn—Mary, DEAD!

He awakes with a shriek, and sits up with his back against the black rock.

His hand touches something cold. It is a skull, and he shudders as he thrusts it away.

But is he awake? He lifts his fettered hands and rubs his eyes.

He gazes in terror at someone that is sitting, just as he is, with his back against the wall—and asleep.

The rough dress is all disarranged, and the brown hands are covered with blood. It is an awful vision.

He shuts his eyes a moment, but when he opens them again the man is still there! The terror!

The morning sun is glimmering in and falling directly on the awful sleeping face.

He sits bolt upright now and leans forward.

"Kaloomah!" he cries. "Kaloomah!"

And his own voice seems to belong to some spirit behind those prison walls.

But the terror awakes.

And the eyes of the two men meet.

"Don Pedro! You here?"

"Kaloomah. I am."

# CHAPTER XXIX—EASTWARD HO! FOR MERRIE ENGLAND

Captain Roland St. Clair, as he was called by his men, was busy along with Dick and Bill in superintending the sending-off of all heavy baggage downstream, when a man came up and saluted him.

"Well, Harris?"

"The prisoner Peter desires to speak with you, sir, in the presence of two witnesses. He wished me to request you to bring paper, pen, and ink. It is his desire that you should take his deposition."

"Deposition, Harris? But the man is not dying."

"Well, perhaps not, sir. I only tell you what he says."

"I will be in his cell in less than twenty minutes, Harris."

"Dick," said Roland, at the appointed time, "there is some mystery here. Come with me, and you also, Bill."

"What I have to say must be said briefly and quickly," said Peter, sitting up. "I will not give myself the pain," he added, "to think very much about the past. It is all too dark and horrible. But I make this confession, unasked for and being still in possession of all my faculties and reasoning power."

He spoke very slowly, and Dick wrote down the confession as he made it.

"I am guilty, gentlemen. Dare I say 'with extenuating circumstances'? That, however, will be for you to consider. As the matter stands I do not beg for my life, but rather that you should deal with me as I deserve to be treated.

"Death, believe me, gentlemen, is in my case preferable to life. But listen and judge for yourselves, and if parts of my story need confirmation, behold yonder is Kaloomah, and he it was whom I hired to carry your adopted sister away, where in all human probability she could never more be heard of again. Have you got all that down?"

"I have," said Dick.

"But," said Roland, "what reason had you to take so terrible a revenge on those who never harmed you, if revenge indeed it was?"

"It was not revenge. What I did, I did for greed of gold. Listen.

"I was happy in England, and had I only been content, I might now have been married and in comfort, but I fell, and am now the heart-broken villain you see before you.

"You know the will your uncle made, Mr. St. Clair?"

"I have only heard of it."

"It was I who copied it for my master, the wretched solicitor.

"I stole that copy and re-copied it, and sold it to the only man whom it could benefit, and that was your Uncle John."

"My Uncle John? He who sent you out to my poor, dear father?"

"The same. But let me hurry on. The real will is still in possession of the solicitor, and it gives all the estates of Burnley Hall, in Cornwall, to John, in the event of Peggy's death."

"I begin to see," said Dick.

"My reward was to have been great, if I managed the affair properly. I have never had it, and, alas! I need it not now.

"But," he continued, "your villainous uncle was too great a coward to have Peggy murdered. His last words to me on board the steamer before I sailed were: 'Remember—not one single drop of blood shed.'

"I might have done worse than even I did, but these were the words that instigated my vile plot, of which I now most heartily repent. All I had to do was to get apparent proof of Peggy's death."

"And my Uncle John now holds the estates of Burnley Hall? Is that so?"

"He does. The solicitor could not help but produce the will, on hearing of Peggy's capture and death.

"That, then, is my story, gentlemen. Before Heaven I swear it is all true. It is, moreover, my deposition, for I already feel the cold shadow of death creeping over me. Yes, I will sign it."

He did so.

"I makee sign too," said Kaloomah.

"That is the man whom I hired to do the deed," said Peter again.

And Kaloomah made his mark.

"I feel easier now, gentlemen" continued Peter. "But leave me a while. I would sleep."

————

Kaloomah had all a savage's love for the horrible, and he was merely an interested spectator of the tragedy that followed.

Between him and Peter lie two poison-tipped arrows.

At first Peter looks at them like one dazed. Then he glances upwards at the glorious sunshine streaming in through the opening.

Nearer and nearer he now creeps to those arrows!

Nearer and nearer!

Now he positions them with his manacled hands.

Then strikes.

In half an hour's time, when Burly Bill entered the cave to inform the prisoners that it was time for them to be on the road, he started back in horror.

Peter, fearfully contorted, lay on the floor of the cave, dead.

————

Some weeks after this the party found themselves once more near to the banks of the rapid Madeira.

Everything had gone well with those captains and peons whom they had left behind, and now every preparation was made to descend the stream with all possible speed, consonant with safety.

They had taken Kaloomah thus far, lest he should return and bring another army to attack them.

And now a kind of drum-head court-martial was held on this wild chief, at which even Charlie and Benee were present.

"I really don't see," said Roland, "what good has come of saddling ourselves with a savage."

"No, I agree with you, Roll," said Dick. "Peter has gone to his account, and really this Kaloomah has been more sinned against than he has sinned."

"What would you advise, Bill?"

"Why, I'd give him a rousing kick and let him go."

"And you Benee?"

"I go for hangee he."

"Charlie, what would you do?"

Charlie was smiling and rubbing his hands; it was evident he had formulated some plan that satisfied himself.

"I tie dat savage to one biggee stake all by de ribber, den watch de 'gator come, chumpee, chumpee he."

But a more merciful plan was adopted. Kaloomah evidently expected death, but when Roland himself cut his bonds and pointed to the west, the savage gave just one wild whoop and yell, and next moment he had disappeared in the forest.

———

Were I beginning a story instead of ending one, I should not be able to resist the temptation to describe that voyage down the beautiful Madeira.

It must suffice to say that it was all one long and happy picnic.

Just one grief, however, had been Peggy's at the start. Poor Dixie, the pony, must be left behind.

She kissed his forehead as she bade him good-bye, and her face was wet with tears as she turned her back to her favourite.

Roland did what he could to comfort her.

"Dixie will soon be as happy as any horse can be," he said. "He will find companions, and will live a long, long time in the wilds of this beautiful land. So you must not grieve."

———————

There are times when people in this world are so inexpressibly happy that they cannot wish evil to happen even to their greatest enemies. They feel that they would like every creature, every being on earth, to be happy also.

Surely it is with some such spirit that angels and saints in heaven are imbued.

Had you been on board the steamship *Panama* as she was swiftly ploughing her way through the wide blue sea that separates Old England from South America, from Pará and the mouths of the mighty Amazon, you could not have been otherwise than struck with the evident contentment and happiness of a group of saloon passengers there. Whether walking the quarter-deck, or seated on chairs under the awning, or early in the morning surrounding their own special little breakfast-table, pleasure beamed in every eye, joy in every face.

Who were they? Listen and I shall tell you.

There was Roland, Dick, Roland's sweet-faced mother, Peggy; and last, but certainly not least in size at all events, there was dark-skinned jolly-looking Burly Bill himself.

But Burly Bill did not obtrude his company too much on the younger folks. He was fond of walking on the bridge and talking to the officer on duty. Fond, too, of blowing a cloud from his lips as they dallied with his great meerschaum. Fond of telling a good story, but fonder still of listening to one, and often chuckling over it till he appeared quite apoplectic.

There was someone else on board who must be mentioned. And this was Dixie, the pony!

Did he remain on the banks of the Madeira? Not he. For by some means or other he found his way—so marvellous is the homing instinct in animals— back to the old plantation long before Roland and his little army, and was the first to run out to meet Peggy and get a kiss on his soft warm snout.

Need I add that Brawn was one of the passengers? And a happy dog he was, and always ready for a lark when the sailors chose to throw a belaying-pin for him.

Dick had had a grief to face when he returned.

His uncle was dead. So he determined—as did Roland with his plantation—to sell off and return to England, for a time at all events.

The two estates are now worked by a "Company Ltd.", but Jake Solomons is head overseer.

Benee, who has married his "moon-dream", little Weenah, is second in command, and right merry of a morning is the boom and the song of the old buzz-saw.

———

So happy, then, were Roland and Dick and Peggy that they concluded they would not be too hard on wicked Uncle John.

This wicked Uncle John went into retirement after the arrival of our heroes and heroine. He might have been sent into retirement of quite a different sort if Roland had cared to press matters.

Peggy got all her own again. She is now Mrs. Temple, and Dick and she are beloved by all the tenantry—yes, and by all the county gentry and farmer folks round and round.

I had almost forgotten to say a last word about Beeboo. She is Mrs. Temple's chief servant, and a right happy body is Beeboo, and Burly Billy is estate manager.

Now, if any of my readers want a special treat, let him or her try to get an invitation to spend Christmas at Burnley Old Hall.